THE
GOOD
GERMAN

Also by Dennis Bock

Going Home Again
The Communist's Daughter
The Ash Garden
Olympia

DENNIS BOCK

THE
GOOD
GERMAN

A NOVEL

PATRICK CREAN EDITIONS
HarperCollins*Publishers*Ltd

The Good German
Copyright © 2020 by Dennis Bock

Published by Patrick Crean Editions, an imprint of HarperCollins Publishers Ltd

First edition

HarperCollins books may be purchased for educational, business or sales promotional use through our Special Markets Department.

HarperCollins Publishers Ltd
Bay Adelaide Centre, East Tower
22 Adelaide Street West, 41ST Floor
Toronto, Ontario, Canada
M5H 4E3

www.harpercollins.ca

Library and Archives Canada Cataloguing in Publication
Title: The good German : a novel / Dennis Bock.
Names: Bock, Dennis, 1964- author.
Identifiers: Canadiana (print) 20200237349 | Canadiana (ebook) 20200237411 |
ISBN 9781443460972 (softcover) | ISBN 9781443460989 (ebook)
Classification: LCC PS8553.O42 G66 2020 | DDC C813/.54—dc23

Printed and bound in the United States of America
LSC/H 9 8 7 6 5 4 3 2

For my mother, who shared stories

Here we are, trapped in the amber of the moment.
There is no why. —Kurt Vonnegut, *Slaughterhouse-Five*

PROLOGUE

Lina Teufel was given no choice in the matter on the day Sister Evelyn came to tell her that the newborn's mother had died in the night. They stood in silence at the top of the basement stairs for a moment, both unnerved by this tragic turn, and when the baby shifted in Sister Evelyn's arms, Lina felt the warm, tingling sensation of her milk begin to let down, even though she'd nursed her own son just two hours earlier, before making her way to the hospice.

She took the baby and followed Sister Evelyn upstairs to where the child's blind father waited. He stood when they entered the room and nodded as the sister informed him that a wet nurse had been found, then seated himself again without a word. The cataracts in his eyes were pearl-like and frightening and gave him the look of a haunted man.

The child was fussing now, rooting with hungry complaint. Sister Evelyn gestured for Lina to sit, and once she had, on the backless divan opposite the father, Lina unclasped the top buttons of her uniform and raised the newborn to her breast.

As the baby fed, Lina watched and pitied the man and wondered about his wife, the young mother who'd died in the night—somewhere in the hospice, she imagined, perhaps in a room only a few doors down the hall. She remembered the birth of her own son, so terrifying and difficult, and thought it more likely than not that the poor woman had died of some complication in childbirth from which she herself, for no reason she knew, had been spared.

The newborn's arms came free from the swaddling then, and Sister Evelyn, standing close, reached forward to replace the blanket, but not before Lina saw the child's disfigured hands, clawed and twisted and startling enough to cause her to retract and to gasp audibly.

The father rose from his chair.

Lina looked to Sister Evelyn with pleading eyes, the tumble of shock and horror and compassion crashing through her, but the sister only crossed herself and gestured once again that she was to proceed. And so began the nursing that would continue on into the autumn, always in the room that looked south over the rolling grounds of the estate and the shingle beach at the foot of the property. As much as possible Lina tried to avoid looking at the father. He was always in the room with her, silent as she nursed his daughter. Through the window she watched the big ships at anchor beyond the harbour, and on clear mornings she studied the horizon that she'd been told was America, just twenty miles across the lake.

She did not hate the baby at first, but nor did she love her, too sore from the hard gums that pulled at her day and night, and worse yet from the scrubbing she submitted herself to after nursing the sickly infant. She learned to feed her in tandem with her son, whom she fed first thing in the morning and upon her return home in the evening.

Port Elizabeth was flooded with men back from the war. She felt their resentment in the town's quiet streets when she walked to and from work. She felt it when she saw them standing in breadlines and at soup kitchens near the harbour where the troop transports from Plymouth and Liverpool and Bristol had released them, deep in the heart of the continent. She heard the condemnation in the catcalls and insults they yelled after her. She felt it in her bones. Go back to where you came from, you're not wanted here, they said.

She didn't blame these returning soldiers for the prejudice they held against her, or the last of those in town like her who'd yet to be rounded up and sent away, as she feared she'd be if she failed in her duties at Mercy House.

She spoke German only at home with her husband, never at the hospice. Once, she let slip a German phrase as the child nursed, and for a full week afterwards she worried that the blind father would report the infraction, still unaware as she was that they held this language in common. Nor did she know how he longed to tell her that he himself was trapped here in this town, in this residence for the blind—not as she was, as a servant, but as someone who'd been obliged to escape his past.

He was not English, she knew that, but she was unable to place his accent on the few occasions she heard him speak with a sister. It suggested none of the romance languages, certainly not Portuguese—she'd already heard too much of that in her young life—and so she decided he was a Swede or Norwegian or Dane who'd found himself in London on the day of the bomb and later shipped here from one of the evacuee stations she'd heard about. She decided too that he was a decent man, for he seemed not to judge her or to detest her the way the other patients did. He was always proper and polite—silently, for they never spoke—though she had no rights or privileges at all, here in this house where not even her body was her own.

He was twenty or more years her senior, not yet fifty, perhaps, but the spirit seemed to have all but gone out of him, and how could it be otherwise, she thought, a blind man with a dead wife, and the poor child the way she was.

Lina did not tell her husband about her added duties as the child's wet nurse at Mercy House. Born and raised in this country, and German only on his mother's side, he'd not suffered as she had since arriving in Canada. In the odd calculus that was her ability to know and to judge those around her, she felt he'd not yet earned the position from which she viewed the world and its array of miseries. She was not cynical, simply a realist, she might have stated when she began to look upon his optimism with condescension and, when the issue finally began to rise between them, contempt. There was no note of falsehood about him. It was simply his incomplete grasp of the real world that gnawed at her, now only a year into their marriage. She'd loved him for this at first, charmed by those qualities that would soon irritate her. Of course you could not argue the fact that life amounted to little more than a cruel test of the will, all so perfectly articulated by the war that had brought them together. Nor did he try. Her husband was no fool, she knew that. In fact, he was in many respects more able than her, confident and practical, and warm in a way she wasn't with their son. But it was his naïveté that failed her understanding of the times they lived in, and for which she began to silently condemn him.

By midsummer she and the blind father had exchanged a word or two—simple, formal, and always in their broken English. The shame and embarrassment she'd felt during those first feedings were no longer there. Even the sight and touch of the child's grotesque hands did not repel her anymore. She always washed her breast after the child was finished, though, continuing the practice into the last days of summer, but not so rigorously as she once had. The father sometimes held his daughter's hand while she nursed, his own fingers hovering close to Lina's breast, and in time this too did not bother her.

Every day he wanted to tell her that he didn't belong here, not rightfully, and to share what they had in common—their language, their history of betrayals—and though he was so much older than her, he imagined they could speak as equals, each affected in their own way by the war. He wanted to tell her about the solitude and the sorrow that tore at his heart every night, and the fear he felt at the thought of raising this child now without her mother. He'd known only deprivation and survival these last years. It was the simple things he yearned for. He needed to hear and to speak his own language again, and to share the truth of his story with someone who'd not judge or report or condemn him. Once, through a closed door, he heard her singing a German lullaby to his daughter. He paused before entering the room, taken by such profound nostalgia and remorse that he almost wept.

He wondered why this silent young woman who'd done nothing to deserve the fate that trapped her here seemed to harbour no resentment towards him or his sickly daughter. But the secret stayed unspoken between them as the late-summer days grew shorter and the early-afternoon sun drew its shadows over the estate lawns. Sometimes he liked to imagine the surprise she'd feel if he suddenly spoke to her in the language they shared—the immediate thrill that would seize her, and then the confusion, and at last the fear when he finally told her his incredible story.

1960

My brother and I were always in school when the scientists came to make their annual inspection at Mercy House. It was never easy for German kids like us to cut class in those days. But this was something we wouldn't have missed for the world. We'd meet at the bike racks at recess when word came that the trucks they always arrived in had been spotted on Main Street and ride down to the old mansion by the lake, where we'd find a dozen or more boys already milling around, waiting nervously for the show to begin.

Mercy House was set a short distance back from the gravel laneway that our teachers liked to refer to as Sanctuary Road, this for the fact that the hospice was home to the last of the evacuees who'd been delivered to our town years ago to receive the sort of medical attention that was in short supply in England after the war. We had our own names for that narrow tree-lined drive that we didn't share with our teachers. Blind Man's Alley was one. Or Radiation Row. These were some of the place names my brother, Thomas, and I lifted from the comic books we liked to read back then. But we'd never seen a comic book with a house as mysterious or frightening as this one.

It was an old English-style country mansion half-covered in creepers and ivy and bordered on three sides (the fourth opened onto Lake Ontario) by a mossy fieldstone wall just high enough to make it difficult for kids like us to peer over. On those chilly spring afternoons after ditching school we laid our bikes at the side of the road and found a foothold on the wall, where we watched and waited for the inspectors to begin unloading the two big canvas-topped ZIL-157s they'd parked at the bottom of the drive, not far from the brass-knockered door that was the main entrance to the house. Those trucks, like so many other things we depended on back then, were a gift from the Soviet Union, our lifeline and protector against the threats that surrounded us now, since the end of that disastrous war. We saw and felt the Russian presence all around us in those days—in household appliances and automobiles and in the doctors who served in the medical centres in town. Usually the inspectors spoke decent English, but on this particular day, mixed with the sound of the waves rolling over the pebbled shore at the bottom of the property, we heard them speaking their impenetrable language as they donned protective suits and retrieved their tools from the backs of the trucks, none more expressive or alarming than the Geiger counters they pulled like swords from their grey cloth sheaths.

These strange devices were silent as a stick of wood when we first saw them but crackled to life when they were deployed over a certain patch of ground, sending a bolt of excitement through our hearts. Each man had one of these instruments. It was a small grey box connected by a cord to a wand that, from where we watched, peering over the stone wall, looked like some variation on the clothes iron our mother used on our shirts and pants. We couldn't see the faces of the inspectors who wielded these tools. They wore black rain slickers and boots and gloves and white masks over their noses and mouths.

After sweeping the grounds (this was the word some of the older boys used to describe the process—*sweeping*), they filed up the stone steps to where they were greeted by two nursing sisters and a man dressed in a dark suit. From this distance we had no clear view of the faces of those who greeted the visitors, but we knew them to be the keepers of the house. They passed documents back and forth for signing, and then the door was closed behind them and there, inside the hospice, they stayed for an hour or more performing duties that set our imaginations on a fearful tear. Now and then one of the men came back outside carrying a grey sample bag in each hand, or to retrieve an item from the back of one of the trucks. It was an agonizing hour we passed as we waited, our anticipation holding us rooted like trees to the ground.

When the team emerged from the house they stowed their gear, stripped off their protective suits, and got back into their trucks. The ZIL-157s were thunderously loud things, like the war they'd been harvested from. When their motors were turned over, the air vibrated, and as they rolled through the gates, one of the men might lower the passenger-side window and call out something to us in Russian, which sent a shiver down our spines. No one among us understood what was said. But we all knew enough to be captured by the strangeness of the afternoon.

We spat nervously and rubbed our hands together while we watched the trucks drive away up the road. The older boys smoked cigarettes and bounced the front tires of their Spitfire two-speed racers against the gravel, and after the trucks turned right on Main Street they made brave declarations about Queen and Country and promised they'd rather crunch a cyanide pill between their teeth than let themselves get turned into a mass of human jelly like the poor souls trapped behind those stone walls. Shaken and exhilarated, Thomas and I kept our mouths shut and slipped away unnoticed.

We rode our bikes back to school and tried to disappear into the anonymity of our day, hopeful that our teachers would forgive the lies we'd rehearsed to explain our absences (they never did), and over the days to come we waited for the local paper to publish the results of the inspection. We knew what they'd say. It was the same every year—the hospice and grounds declared safe, no traces of radiation found. But we could not be tricked, for the certainty of our beliefs bordered on the superstitious. What we knew in our hearts could not be so easily dismissed. We knew what we'd seen and heard—those Geiger counters chattering as clearly as crickets in a garden. There was no question you'd burn like an egg in a frying pan if you got too close to that property for too long, and though the poor blind souls holed up in there might be taking their sweet time dying, dying they were, and no one could do a thing about it.

The fact that our mother had done her Service of Atonement at Mercy House and survived the ordeal didn't allay our fears or disarm our superstitions. It gave us a more immediate and intimate connection to its history than the other boys had, though. We knew its background, too, of course—that, for example, the Order of the Sisters of Saint Joseph had come up from Pennsylvania in 1847 to meet the first waves of Irish Famine immigrants that were arriving then in their miserable coffin ships to the north shore of Lake Ontario. We knew they'd tended to the sick and the dying in the fever sheds on Richmond Street in Toronto, only an hour west, and at the Hotel Dieu and in MacDonald Park in Kingston—two hours east—many themselves succumbing to the typhus. Yet despite these losses the Order continued on in the province for years; and in 1944, five generations later, it acquired the abandoned Raymar estate in the town where we grew up and turned it into the hospice for those blinded on that terrible day in London, and where our mother had worked for the first five years of her new life in Canada.

She was two months pregnant with my brother when her service began in November 1944 and had no training or particular interest in health care or the blind, specifically. There was a position to be filled at Mercy House after the passing of the Atonement Act. It was as simple as that, she said. As a non-preferred immigrant she was removed from her private employment as a domestic and placed at the hospice to serve the mandatory term that befell any German newcomer back then. She reported to the house carrying the one small suitcase that contained her few possessions, and there she stayed for the duration of her term, enjoying only the limited freedom of spousal privilege—meaning she could live off-premises with her new husband. The sisters and medical staff who ran their lives referred to her and the others as atonement girls, those young German women whose guilt by association was never in doubt. They were expected to perform their duties unfailingly and in absolute silence, and to have no contact whatever with the wards of the house.

At its peak as many as ninety people resided at Mercy House, but my mother saw very little of them. She spent her time in the kitchen and laundry doing jobs that kept her confined to the basement and scullery, far removed from the patients who would have protested, and perhaps violently so, against the idea of one of the German girls coming anywhere near them. Her state of mind worsened when she finally confirmed her pregnancy. She would have accepted any posting to get away from the illness that was in those early years slowly emptying the house—even a posting in the dangerous far north, she told us, anything to leave from there—but the nursing sisters, unmoved by her condition, turned down her repeated requests for a transfer, unwavering in their determination that all penitents must be made to pay their due.

A second German girl had stayed on at Mercy House during a pregnancy, and her child had been born with no deformities whatever. This young woman had put her faith in the folk remedies for the prevention and cure for radiation sickness that were widely held at the time. If you stuck to the protocols, she told my mother, the unborn would stand at least a decent chance. She'd taken powdered charcoal and bee pollen in her tea during her pregnancy, liberally spread sunscreen on her abdomen and face and arms before every shift, and scrubbed herself head to toe—sometimes to the point of bleeding—at the end of the day.

As determined as she was terrified, my mother followed a similar regimen during her pregnancy with my brother. She wore gloves when handling the laundry—bedsheets and pillow cases were thought to be especially hazardous— and washed her hands in bleach a half-dozen times a day. She did everything possible to protect my brother from the terrors she and our father saw on *The World in Action* reels that screened ahead of the feature at the Playhouse on Main Street, where later as a family we watched the Vincent Price and Boris Karloff movies we loved so much. Over the span of her first pregnancy, and later, with me, she went to bed every night fearing the worst, her hands stripped and burning from the cruel protocols she subjected herself to. It seemed her efforts were not in vain. In May 1945 Thomas was born healthy and perfect, thank goodness, and on a bright August morning two years later I followed, kicking and screaming, into this strange new world.

THE HOUSE WE LIVED in looked like any other house in our neighbourhood. The only difference was the number that identified us as a German family, 169061-4, painted on our front door. It can be said we lived in a decent house, though, there was that at least, and for this we were grateful. Ours was a company house similar in size and construction to all the others on our street—a one-and-a-half-storey, three-bedroom bungalow with a sheet-asphalt driveway that disappeared into the closed confines of a single-bay garage. In our unfinished basement we had a new Saratov oil furnace; in the backyard we maintained the sort of small garden that people had called a victory garden during the war but was now known as a liberty garden. We lived in this house because our father was employed by the shipbuilding concern that owned most everything else in town and whose steam whistle we heard blowing at the end of the day's shift on the far side of the river that divided the town of Port Elizabeth into east and west.

As slow and brown as the catfish we caught from its muddy banks, the Burnt River had been crucial in the making of our town. Its only set of riffles was up near Old Mill Road, just ankle-deep at that point, and at its most ambitious it might have spanned fifty feet and run no deeper than ten or twelve. But the Burnt (as it was known) had been used to float logs from the county's earliest cuttings, soon stripped bare in the building of the British fleet in the 1800s; later its modest powers were harnessed by the mills that rose on its banks. The vast barley fields where the oaks had once stood sent their harvests south to the harbour, from which point the malted grain was poured into the cargo holds of topsail schooners that sailed southwest for the Niagara River or east towards the Saint Lawrence and on to England. The tanneries, too, took a foothold here, on the west side of the harbour, and the pelts taken from the surrounding woodland became purses and shoes and carriage tops. Finally, in 1908, with the launch of Henry Ford's Tin Lizzie in Detroit, our small town experienced another of its many booms, providing leather for hundreds of car seats and roofs per day. No enterprise here was stronger or more firmly rooted than the Chisolm Shipyards Company. Even through the Great Depression the town managed to keep its young men employed, its families fed and clothed and housed. Once the war started, the antiquated tanneries and mills were knocked down, the shipyard rapidly expanded, and waves of men soon came searching for opportunity as the war quadrupled the size of our population in under a year.

The Chisolm Company owned our house, as I say, and the lot it was built on, as it did most others in town. We shopped in their stores and played in their parks and attended their schools. We were a company family living in a company town. Everything we did depended on the yard. On average we built two cruisers a year, and once three—in the year of the Suez Crisis—and dry-docked and repaired a dozen more, and we saw ourselves transformed into a town of old men, women, and children when the Royal Navy came to port—the names HMS *Montgomery,* the *Excelsior,* the *Liverpool* rang magically in my ears—for there was not a single working man to be seen in the streets at such times, each and every last one called in to work until the vessel in question was shipshape again.

The hull steel used by the yard came from the Stelco Company of Hamilton, Ontario, situated at the western end of the lake—thirty or so miles as the crow flies, fifty by road—and on a clear night you could see the glow of the smelters and blast furnaces when you stood at the bottom of our street, just three blocks from home, the sky in that direction lit by fires that appeared to me in my child's wonder as a constellation of stars. In all seasons we heard the heavy rumble of freight trains as they rolled through town to feed the shipyard and the Hamilton steel mills, and from our vantage on the Bridge of Heroes, a half-mile up from where the Burnt River emptied into Lake Ontario and over which we crossed on the days we met our father at the shipyard gates, we saw the vast expanse of building docks and cranes and rail lines and the dozens of ships stacked like islands to the horizon as they waited to make port. Ten blocks back in the direction of home was the pocket of trees that was our neighbourhood and the enduring misery of Mercy House.

OUR FATHER'S NAME WAS Howard Teufel. The fact that he'd been kept away from the war when there still was an actual war to fight had caused him many sleepless nights when he was a young man. In 1940 he was twenty years old, healthy and strong but for the diabetes that was his category-one exemption. He visited the recruiting office in his hometown of Kingston, Ontario, half a dozen times to talk the duty officer into turning a blind eye to his damning medical report. On each occasion he was denied the opportunity to prove himself in the way so many other local boys were doing. He hated the Nazis as much as everyone else did, he assured anyone who'd listen. But he was a coward in the eyes of those who saw him striding down a Kingston street at the height of the war, a *white-feather case*, they called it. And for this he was burdened by shame until the day his fortunes finally turned in June 1943, when he was recruited by the Corps of Engineers out of Petawawa, Ontario, and put to work on the greatest engineering project of the war.

The expansion of the Saint Lawrence Seaway had begun by then, first at Côte Ste Catherine and later at various other points along the length of that thousand-mile-long waterway. He was trained on a single-bucket grab-dredger, which he soon mastered, and on May 1, 1944, the day he turned twenty-four, the final lock was opened and christened with the passage of the HMS *Victorious* as she made her way upriver into the heart of North America and the safety of the Great Lakes. After he was processed out of the Corps that summer, he came to Port Elizabeth and found a position as a crane operator at the Chisolm Shipyards, which were then expanding as a result of the Miracle Canal, so dubbed by the national press—this for the fact that the British Navy now had safe harbour in which to shelter from the stinging U-boat wolf-pack attacks that had plagued the North and South Atlantic since the start of the war. He took a room near the docks once he was hired on, and on Sunday afternoons he strolled the quiet green of Gairloch Gardens in the east end of town in hopes of silencing the clamour of industry that continued on in his head long after his workweek was ended.

He introduced himself to my mother after he saw her feeding a family of mallards one fall afternoon in his first year here. She had a shy, pretty smile that immediately drew him to her, he said, but she was cautious and halting as she struggled to understand his intentions. English was still a struggle for her, and when he offered to speak German, and then did so, he informed her that, yes, he was Canadian through and through, but that his mother had come over from Hamburg in 1919, and that German was the language she'd used at home when he was growing up. He learned that day that my mother's aunt had put her on board a ship called the *St. Louis* bound for Cuba in 1938. After the port authority in Havana turned them away for no reason she knew, the ship sailed northeast for the Canaries, and finally, after sitting off Tenerife for three months, the Portuguese government granted them permission to call in at Ponta Delgada, in the Azores. There, at the age of fourteen, my mother was deloused, interrogated, and placed in the internment camp that became her home for two years, until Canada, on humanitarian grounds—most of the passengers on the *St. Louis* were juveniles—opened its doors in 1943, only a few months before our parents met that afternoon at Gairloch Gardens. She and my father spent the rest of that day walking the grounds, avoiding talk of the dangerous heritage they shared, which he'd done his best to hide since the start of the war.

MY PARENTS PULLED MY brother from school for a full week in October 1953, the year he began first grade, when news broke that Germany had decided to up the ante by testing their first hydrogen bomb in the Libyan desert. In an instant the Doomsday Clock was moved to one minute before midnight, and violent anti-German protests swept the nation. My mother watched the street from the living room window in the days that followed that test, always fearful that the roving mobs would turn their attention to our house. The few remaining German-owned businesses that had survived the attempt to remove the German population from the economy were torched—the Commonwealth First Decree having been modelled after what had been done to the Jews in Europe a decade earlier—and my mother and father, ever fearful, locked our doors and waited for the War Measures Act to return order to the streets. Even my father stayed away from work that week as our town buckled under the protests after Libya. Thomas was old enough to remember the crowds and the chanting and the smoke rising from the Vogel & Sons hardware store on Main Street. But I can't claim to have an accurate recollection of those times, still cocooned as I was in the pleasant ignorance of childhood. Nor do I remember the day shortly after when news came that a Soviet hydrogen bomb had been successfully tested in Kazakhstan, as Sakharov's atomic bomb had been nine years earlier, just three weeks after Germany had deployed the only bomb it had over London. With that new Soviet hydrogen bomb, the brief advantage held by Berlin in 1953 evaporated in an instant, as it had in 1944, and the balance of power once again guaranteed that neither Germany nor the Soviets were willing to violate the truce that prevailed. And so, for now, here in this socialist northern enclave, we were safe.

THROUGH ALL THIS I saw no reason to believe that we weren't like any other family. Normal is what you know and see every day when you're a child, and to my mind we were ordinary and undeserving of notice or special treatment, one way or the other. Our routines and rituals seemed to fall in line with the typical Canadian family's. As I imagined everyone else in town did, we gathered in front of our new Soviet-made Izumrud 201/203 television to watch the hockey game beamed in from Maple Leaf Gardens or the Montreal Forum on Saturday nights. Often the picture was fuzzy, and always blue on top, reddish in the middle, and green at the bottom, this a result of the special plastic laminate our father had purchased and adhered to the television screen to bring some colour to our viewing experience. The miracle of television was still something to behold, its imperfections as magical as the thing itself. We loved the Leafs and disliked the Canadiens and watched in awe when the Soviet national team swept the 1958 exhibition series that riveted the whole country. The picture didn't matter as long as the broadcast didn't cut out suddenly, as it often did in those days. But this too helped me believe we were participants in what could be called normal life. The same interruptions, shortages, and power outages burdened us as they did everyone else in town. We built snow forts and rode our toboggan down Jackson's Hill in winter and pedalled our bikes in summer and lived in a neighbourhood whose houses looked warm and comfortable and safe. In the fall we harvested vegetables from our liberty garden and, like so many families did back then, we went on country drives, in the '38 Chevy Deluxe Coupe my father was so proud of.

Sometimes we drove as far north as Simcoe County, where our parents talked about renting a cabin one day. I liked to watch the way my mother might straighten my father's collar as he drove, or touch his hair when he spoke with measured optimism about the shape of our future, or praise the car he'd finally managed to save enough to purchase second-hand from a man at the shipyard. Ours was one of the few American automobiles you still saw on the road. If you had a car it was usually a Lada or a Moskvitch, both sturdy enough, manufactured as they were with the Russian winter in mind. Our old Chevy was beyond exotic compared to those Everyman cars. You just didn't see them anymore. I don't think my father cared much about being seen in an unusual car, though.

It was more a question of what that automobile repre-sented about the way America used to be before everything got turned upside down. He usually looked pleased when he drove it, and often my mother's fingers settled on his shoul-der for a mile or two, the old Chevy chugging along, and for me this display of affection between my parents was as good as or better than renting a cabin up north or meeting him at the shipyard after the steam whistle sounded, for it told of a confidence between them that made it easier to disregard the troubling signs that had finally begun to make themselves known to me.

Perhaps the one sign that puzzled me most in those early days was not the number painted on our front door—mistaken at that early age for our home address, added to the more recognizable street number 115 tacked onto a front porch post—but the nervousness that plagued our father when he was in public. At home he was calm and happy, or at least he seemed that way to me—the sort of father who pulled a coin from your ear on your birthday or played Herb Alpert songs on his old dented trumpet. But in the street he was always on guard. "Come on now, William, get a move on," he'd say, throwing a glance over his shoulder. He didn't associate with men from the shipyard as far as I can remember, and I have no recollection of visitors calling at our house when I was a boy. At the annual company picnic he never played pickup baseball or talked with the men in the beer tent where so many other fathers seemed to collect. He sat with us instead; and once, after I made the mistake of speaking the wrong language, he raised a finger to his lips and reminded me that outside the home we were to speak only English.

At the end of the day, as we settled into our beds after one such picnic, Thomas told me it was the war that dictated the use of the languages we spoke and where we were allowed to speak them. Everything was about the war, he said, even the number painted on our front door. Everyone hated us the same way you hated the monster in a monster movie. I'd see for myself soon enough, once school started that fall. I remembered no war, only stories that told of our father's regret at not having served. It seemed far-fetched that something that had happened outside the span of my own life could hold such harsh sway over our town and family. Thomas reached for the flashlight at his bedside and pressed it to the underside of his chin.

"It's a cold war now, stupid, that's what they call it," he said. The term *cold war* was new to me. Icebergs and snow-swept plains and howling winds came to mind. "So you'd better get used to not having any friends at all. We watch films at school. You'll see them, too. They blame us for everything."

"Us?" I said.

"The Germans."

"What happens in the films?"

He scanned the ceiling with the flashlight beam. We'd strung half a dozen model airplanes up there, on fishing line, in a perpetual dogfight that moved only slightly when a breeze came through the window.

"Nothing goes right, anyway," he said.

The beam traced across the ceiling in a cool, steady arc. He knew all there was to know. There could be no reason to doubt what he told me, though no sense could be made of it in my trusting heart. I looked up to him in every way a little brother could. He was taller and stronger and smarter than I could ever hope to be, and when he told me I'd never have friends in my life I believed him as you believe the crystal ball that speaks the truth to you about your deepest and most shameful secret. He'd already learned something at school called duck-and-cover and knew the location of all the fallout shelters in town, and that in the early days following the war they'd been known as sanctuaries and not shelters. The name made people feel better, he said. It made them feel safer. He even claimed to know by the light in the sky over Hamilton what grade of steel they were baking in the Stelco firepits.

"Maybe you don't want to know what our last name means in German," he said.

"Maybe I do," I said.

Silence fell between us, and he shone the flashlight under his chin again and snapped the setting from white to red.

"Teufel means devil," he said.

Such pronouncements did not frighten me so terribly in the morning as they did at night, and though I learned that our family name did in fact mean in German what he said it did, I chose to believe for as long as I could that we were no different from anyone else. No one had any reason to hate us. I couldn't bear to think of the lonely future that Thomas had predicted for me. I decided that our name was just a sound that came out of your mouth. The childless couple on our street five doors up whom I waved to on occasion, and who always pretended not to see me, were not green, though we

knew them as Mr. and Mrs. Green, and so by that same logic
I assured myself that there was nothing of the devil in us at all.

THE NOTION THAT WE were an ordinary family was tested
on most days once the truth began to come clear to me, but
never more than when our town paused on the sixth day
of August to recall the war that had taken so much from so
many. For us there was no date on the calendar as frightening
as Remembrance Day. What gathered over our house as the
anniversary approached was a gloomy mood that caused our
parents to snap at me and my brother for the smallest infraction. On the day itself we were not permitted to play outside,
not even in our backyard, much less in the street, where the
sight and sound of a couple of German boys would have been
reported to the neighbourhood Citizen Patrol by one or more
of our busybody neighbours. Even if the weather was fine,
which often it was in early August, we didn't so much as step
out onto the front porch until we were ready to walk up to
Chisolm Square, where we took part in the memorial service.

My mother, a seamstress by training, had made the black
suit my father wore on this solemn occasion. She sewed
clothes for us kids, too, which Thomas never failed to com-
plain about. He referred to her creations as immigrant clothing, for her sweaters and winter toques and mittens featured
more than a hint of the place where she'd learned her craft,
and this openly Germanic patterning was seized upon by

most everyone in the schoolyard, including those teachers who did little to conceal their prejudice against us. School was bad enough as it was without our mother painting yet another bull's eye on his back, Thomas said. One year he refused to wear any of it, until our father put a stop to his nonsense, settling the matter once and for all when he told him it was that or go to school wearing no clothes at all.

This suit she'd made was tight now on my father's shoulders and waist—she'd made it when they were newlyweds—and it was plain to see the fit caused him some discomfort. He turned his whole body instead of just his head when he wanted to talk to you, as if he had a stitch in his neck, and he rolled his shoulders and head often, attempting to find a posture that might relieve the stiffness. And so, dressed in our own suit jackets and ties (also crafted by our mother, loosely tailored so that our young bodies might grow into them), we followed our father outside onto the front porch where we waited for her to join us. She was always the last one ready that morning. Our father would check his watch minute by minute as we stood there, looking left and right up and down our street for any sign of the Greens or the Hatchetts or the Friars, or the Citizen Patrol, who might have something to say about this loitering family of irredeemables. Finally, when our mother appeared, grim-faced and steeled with purpose, we came down the front steps together and at last set out for the memorial service.

The smile that had drawn my father's attention on the

afternoon our parents met so long ago was no longer there, in general terms, and less so now on this specific morning. She wore her hair in the style of the day—like the movie stars and the grim ladies you saw on the government posters at school—which gave her a vaguely Slavic look, though her people, as far as she knew, had never ventured beyond the narrow confines of what we believed was her northeastern German bloodline.

It was a short seven blocks to Chisolm Square. On that day it felt like a hundred. We walked in silence most of the way. I did what I could to distract myself. I didn't want to be a bother to my parents. I counted the houses and cars parked in their driveways and listened to the summer sounds that didn't sound like much to me on any other day but today felt personal and heavy with foreboding. Lawn mowers and cars sat idle. Tree frogs and crickets and cicadas filled the morning with their strange songs of courtship and dying. If I was lucky I'd get lost in these sounds for a time. But my reveries never lasted long. Out of an abundance of caution our father would remind us what was expected of his two sons—backs straight, boys, and no staring once we're there—absolutely no staring—and tell us that in attending the service we were letting the whole town know something about who we were. We were on the right side, he'd say, and don't you dare forget that, both of you.

The square was three blocks north of Main Street and one east of Burnt River. It was green and pretty in summer and bordered by houses constructed at the end of the previous century using bricks and stone taken from the ruins of the Marlatt and Armstrong Tannery after it was destroyed by fire in 1870. The houses were much larger than the company house we lived in. Here they were red brick with white gabling and trim and wore black-shingled, double-sloped roofs against the weather and the pine cones that fell from the spruce and fir trees that towered over the neighbourhood.

Many of these houses bore plaques that commemorated their builders or original occupants. They spoke of long-dead carpenters and shipbuilders and merchants, and one, at the southwest corner where we entered the park, told of a Swede named Jacobson who'd run rum from the Port Elizabeth harbour across the lake to Olcott, New York, back in the 1920s. Another memorialized a woman named Gatchel who'd assisted fugitives arrived here from the United States via the Underground Railroad following their escape from slavery in the 1860s. This house, smaller, and predating the tannery fire, was a house of great distinction. One of the tunnels of the Underground Railroad had ended in the basement of this very building, its plaque said, and we were proud to learn that our small town had been one of the many points along the north shore of Lake Ontario where men and women had sought and received refuge in their escape from that great slaving nation to the south.

In all these houses on Remembrance Day the curtains were drawn and the Royal Union Flag, so ubiquitous in those times, was lowered to half-mast. The nervous hum of the crowd gathering at the foot of the towering cenotaph drowned out the cicadas and the birds that had accompanied us on our walk. The names of the local dead were carved below the dates 1939–1944. Above was the inscription:

They Gave Their Lives to Break
the Power of the Sword.

Now as we found our place, far back from the cenotaph, where the resin smell of the trees we stood under startled my nose, the general murmur of a thousand voices filled the day. Fallen pine cones and brittle spruce needles crunched beneath our polished shoes. My father folded his hands together at his waist, the right hand gripping his left wrist, and Thomas and I, diligent and observant, did the same—right gripping left.

Out of the corner of my eye I watched my father, careful not to miss any sign or gesture meant for us, for there were unvoiced protocols and rituals to follow—arms folded just so, head angled like this—and any half-hearted observance would be noticed. We never wavered or slouched. My mother stood next to my father, head down, her arm laced with his. We didn't speak as we waited. In the tree above, even the squirrels seemed to hold off their morning chatter.

The Reverend from Knox Presbyterian at the corner of Charles and Main always presided over the service. He took his position at the base of the cenotaph and raised his hands and offered a prayer. His voice was amplified throughout the park by a public announcement system that only a week earlier might have been used at a county fair. From where we stood back in the trees it sounded weak and tinny, like some faint radio broadcast coming from a far-off city. It was good enough to follow along, though.

The Reverend's sermons told of our town's sacrifice and the enduring hardships of the postwar era and the need to find patience in our hearts and strength in our backs. He spoke of forbearance and industry and the spirit of common purpose as we struggled against the evils of this troubled world; and then he invited the town's dignitaries and veterans to approach. With a soft touch of his wooden cross he blessed them as they bent a knee before him and then laid their wreaths in growing heaps at the base of the cenotaph.

Every year three children were chosen to read out the names of our recent dead. Nearing the end of the service they approached and sang out the names in a way that sounded choral in its beauty and sadness. I imagined what it would feel like to hear my own name sung in this way, to be so revered that the whole town honoured your memory, and that it would almost be worth dying just to know that feeling. It was the legacy of war that got your name remembered in song, and year upon year the list grew, for the war that had ended years earlier seemed not to have ended at all. I wondered too what it would be like to read out those names,

which in the days following the service a team of stonecut-
ters would carve into the ever-growing cenotaph, but neither
I nor my brother was ever afforded the honour, of course.

When the reading of the names was finished, the Reverend presided over a minute of silence, which was then broken
by the mournful blast of the shipyard steam whistle. It blew
louder and longer on this occasion than it did to release a
shift from the yard. My heart trembled as the call pierced the
air, and finally the old Reverend, dressed in his red and black
robes, led us in a prayer:

Vengeance is Mine,
And recompense;
Their foot shall slip in due time;
For the day of their calamity is at hand,
And the things to come
hasten upon them.

We called out "Amen" and saluted, as we'd do every morning when school began that fall, just a short month away—
right fist to the heart, eyes forward, heels together. It was an
impressive sound when the whole town did this as one, a
thousand families or more—and I felt in that instant that
we were a single voice, and that all families were united in
our mourning and our determination, not yet old enough to
understand that we as Germans would never belong.

I was six years old in 1953 when I saw a resident of the

hospice at a memorial service for the first time. Every year thereafter I studied the crowd, searching for that distinctive pairing of a nursing sister and her blind charge. The sight sent a shiver down my spine, yet it was difficult to look away, despite this and our father's warnings not to stare.

By then my brother had shared with me the schoolyard lore that spoke of the degenerative blindness that would strike you if your eyes so much as met theirs, let alone lingered there with the sort of curiosity that possessed me as a boy. It was a hopeless struggle to avert my gaze, try as I did. Returning from Chisolm Square that day I saw my first survivor, I rubbed my eyes so hard that my vision began to blur, and I grew terrified that the blinding had already begun. Once home I splashed warm water in my eyes until my father knocked on the bathroom door and told me that we'd better get cracking, time was running out. Unsure that I'd successfully washed away the curse, I dried my face and joined my family in our preparations for the coming night.

Nearing dusk, after the house was readied, we waited at the kitchen table for it to begin. This was the safest room after the basement, in which our mother was unable to spend more than a few minutes due to the way dark spaces made her feel. The power in the breaker box had been turned off, and we'd filled buckets with water and placed them at the ready by the front door. A single candle flame burned at the centre of the kitchen table, and there we waited for the taverns by the harbour to close for the night.

Ours was the only house they visited on our street on Remembrance Day, but certainly not the only one in town. There were perhaps two dozen German families who'd earned the privilege, as we had, to live where we did, removed from the camp called Little Berlin that held the vast majority of Germans in our town. It had been constructed for those who'd been spared life in any one of the hundreds of internment camps across the country, and they would suffer more than we did. But we could not imagine a fear greater than what we felt as we sat waiting for the crowd to collect in front of our house.

They always gathered slowly at first, in twos and threes, until finally a hundred or more stood on the street a stone's throw from our front door. In the early days, when we were little, our parents tried their best to make us believe this was a harmless ritual, something people did to entertain themselves. But soon enough the look on our father's face made the make-believe difficult to go along with. Now, there was little pretending. He'd rise from his seat and check the front windows, pulling back a strip of curtain. He always carried a baseball bat with him, and our mother always cautioned him to come back before he was spotted. We'd hear the sound of the bat gently slapping into his open palm or tapping against the hardwood floor as he returned to the kitchen, the sound of the mob growing louder and more threatening as the minutes ticked on.

"It's going to be all right, they'll lose interest soon," he'd say, leaning the bat against the panelled wall beside his chair. He'd put his hand on my shoulder and tell us it was just something people did once a year, like Hallowe'en, and there was nothing to be frightened of. It was normal too, he'd say, that they were angry about what had happened during the war; many of them had lost loved ones, after all. They weren't bad people out there, he said, just people stung by loss and hardship and looking for someone to blame.

It was our mother's presence that angered them, not ours, I finally understood. He never said that but eventually I figured this out. The fact that she'd married a man born in this country, and German on only one side—our father's father descending from a long line of Swiss—did not grant her the special status we enjoyed as mixed-race Canadians. It didn't even help that our father had assisted in digging the Miracle Canal that had saved so many ships and lives, or that he now worked at the shipyard, building the frigates and cruisers that would replace those lost in the war. She was German, and that was the end of it. Nothing else mattered. It was of no consequence that she'd served her full term at Mercy House, even risked her health and the health of her unborn children in doing so. It was because of her the mob came; and it was only the purity of my father's defiance that thwarted them.

The light of the bonfire they set on the front lawn was reflected in the glass window of the kitchen stove door. My father was unaware that I could see what was happening out there from this angle. He would have made me sit elsewhere, I'm sure of it. The reflection whirled in the corner of my eye like a firefly. Once more he'd get up, bat in hand, and walk to the living room to check the front window, and my mother, speechless with fear, would grab and hold me to my seat, the haunted expression I can still see these many years later closing over her face like a mask.

Outside, they fed the fire with scraps of lumber and skids and bundles of newspaper and smashed chairs, whatever they could find that would burn. Sometimes the fire leaped to the height of the first branches of the birch tree that grew in our yard. One year there were footsteps on the front porch; another year we heard voices at the side of the house, near the garage, and even once in the backyard. In each case our father gripped the bat in both hands and left the kitchen to investigate, and one night he opened the side door when sounds came from the garage. We heard footsteps rushing back along the driveway in retreat. I remember the terror I felt in my heart, believing my father would go after the man, lured out into the night where he'd fall under the mob's anger. He re-entered the kitchen and stood silently, listening, his pallor turned ghost-white.

Most years the crowd began to thin after midnight. When he was sure the worst of it was over, he stood watch on the front porch for a time, then carried the first bucket down the steps to empty it over the flames.

We brought him refills to soak the coals. It didn't take

long before the kitchen and living room floors were wet and slippery and the smell of the smouldering fire filled the house. Our mother watched from the doorway, arms crossed over her chest. Sometimes a few stragglers stayed behind to observe our quiet industry, too drunk or dispirited to continue with the crowd they'd arrived with. They stood at the edge of the darkness, muttering their slurs. My father would yell at them to move along, sometimes calling out to them by their first name—"The show's over, Mack, on your way," he'd say—and then he'd remove the hatchet that had been driven into the birch tree, as it was every year on Remembrance Day. He'd untie the black ribbon fastened around its handle, drop the ribbon into the dying fire, and throw the hatchet into the open field over the heads of those who lingered there, and then finish up with the bonfire while we went back inside with our mother.

1938–1944

In his own mind and heart Georg Elser was still an ordinary man on the day he entered the shipping department of the Waldenmaier armaments factory, eight years before Mercy House became his home. He was unremarkable to look at and to talk to, indistinguishable from the next man. Everything about his place of employment, too—the small office smelling of mouldy paper and routine—said as much. Stacks of files were pushed up against a grey wall, organized and ready for reference and review. The vague ring of an absent teacup marked a loose leaf of unsigned paper placed squarely in the centre of his desk, and beside it the ledger detailing last night's scheduled deliveries and outgoing shipments awaited his attention.

More than ever he felt the repression and dread that presided over the small town he lived in in the foothills of the Swabian Alps. He found it waiting for him in the morning when he woke; he carried it with him during the day; and at night it circled him in the dark when sleep would not come. It might have been the pity he felt for the men and women he saw every day on his way to the factory in Heidenheim, or in the rheumy eyes of the grandmothers he knelt beside in the church he visited in the evenings where he asked forgiveness for the direction his life was about to take him in. Prayer in his youth had been frequent, but it had been left off for decades, found again only recently. He was a man who spoke into the silence of his heart with the hope that something divine, some moral courage might reside there and guide him. He waited for signs of comradeship or rebellion, some hint of a resistance he could join, but saw none. He pored over broadsheet news bulletins, read the handbills that checkered the stone walls of the old town. And late into the night he listened to dizzying speeches on the wireless while he troubled through the intricacy of the plot that began to weave through his mind.

At thirty-eight he was already too old for soldiering, which he considered no small grace in the accident of his birth. But he did his bit for the coming war. He could not do otherwise. The road he travelled every morning ended at the iron gates of the factory, where he worked with men whose grievances had been mobilized in the service of a new, greater Germany. He wondered who among them felt as he did, enslaved by this false brotherhood as they shaped the shoulder stocks and trigger mechanisms of the next war. But what was needed was a first real act of defiance—not the simple imaginings that came to him more and more in those days. He needed something concrete, as real as the hum of machinery rising and falling and the stutter of rivets that followed him as he passed through this maze: drill presses, metal lathes, everywhere the oiled staccato of industry.

Now he surveyed the ledger, running a finger down the various columns—as he would do six years later in consulting the pocket dictionary on the deck of the *Eendracht* as he sailed for London—and carried the document pressed to his chest to the warehouse in the adjacent building, where he walked between rolls of copper wire and vats of wool and barrels of granular powder and shell casings and crates filled with boxes of detonators and fuses, each item and every last ounce catalogued, accounted for, and marked for its specific time and place.

He set the ledger on the workbench by the window that gave onto a view of a courtyard, crossed the concrete floor and found the crate with the series of numbers he was looking for. He slipped the teeth of the crowbar he'd taken from the bench under the seal and pulled the bar towards his chest. The nails gave way with a dry, high-pitched groaning. He opened the crate and found thirty-six smaller boxes, cardboard, inked, and tightly packed together.

He opened the top of one of the boxes and removed a single detonator. It was a small brass and copper tube not much larger than a pencil, an innocuous-looking thing, inside of which was contained the simple mechanics and basic chemistry of change.

He rolled it in his fingers and imagined the near future as he'd dreamed it so often, free of this scourge, a country where once again he could walk and think and breathe. Here was the idealist in him set aloft, the man of principle who for too long had been fearful of the thought that had been keeping him awake for nights on end. But now the conviction was made real. He held it for a moment to savour the small triumph, the metal cool in his palm, then slipped it into his breast pocket. He returned the resealed box to the crate and tapped it shut again.

For years he'd refused to offer the straight-arm salute that had been taken up by everyone around him. Until now, this small expression of principle had been the only act of defiance he'd been able to muster. In his own mind and heart he would not succumb to the world's ignorance and malevolent nature. But he'd felt powerless. Too often he witnessed the sort of brutality in the streets that left him nauseated with guilt and horror.

Now, with the detonator in his possession, the world seemed alive and available to Elser in a way he'd never known before, and with this moment of courage surging in his chest he felt he had at least a chance to get closer to the sickly heart of the regime than anyone had before him.

For an hour and more that afternoon his hands shook

uncontrollably. He tried to calm his breathing, attempting to get through to the end of the day as if it were any other. The steady hum of machines and men at their work reassured him to some measure. He walked through the various departments as he checked deliveries and outgoing manifests, the detonator still tucked into the folds of his breast pocket. If discovered it would mean the end of him. But the day rolled on without incident. From a scaffolding above the heavy presses that shaped a thousand shell casings an hour he watched hundreds of men working the machines on a factory floor so vast that the end of the production line dissolved in a thick blue haze.

When his shift ended he carried the single detonator out past the guards by the factory's east exit into the failing afternoon light. He tipped his cap as he always did and commented on the weather, which was cold and bracing and dry, then located his bicycle among the many hundreds stationed there at the racks and started down the road to the next village over, where he lived. It was a pleasant ride on most days. He passed through a band of air that smelled of drying hay and thick rich soil. The sun as it hit the hills in the far south bathed the edges of the autumn fields with a cool light that turned his hands the colour of gold. He watched this as he rode home and felt in his heart more alive than the world itself.

AS A BOY HE'D studied the grandfather clock that crowded the sitting room of his family's small home and wondered at the mechanism that marked the steady march of time. He anticipated the moment when the brass pine cone strung from a chain began to move on the quarter hour. The ringing chimes were a joyful sound. It made his heart race. Sometimes it brought him to tears—not for sorrow but for the beauty of such a miraculous instrument. Once, at the age of ten and marked by a curiosity that his father would have regarded as devilment, he opened the clock's glass panel and stilled the pendulum with a finger, this his first experiment with the altering of time.

It was the sort of nuisance his old man would beat him for if he found him out, sure as the forest was green. But the temptation was great and the beatings would come for whatever other reason.

The pendulum resting against his finger, he watched his siblings in the field across from the house through the window. They'd been chasing a red kite, laughing and calling out, but now the kite and the clouds and voices fell still and silent. The entire world paused. Dust motes held in the sun's rays over the windowsill; the games outside froze in the summer heat; time itself ceased its steady beat. He himself continued to move, to breathe, the pulse in his neck beating with expectation. But everything else, nothing. Oh, the world went on, he knew. But in his child's mind—and even in memory as he looked back on that strange day—it was pretty to believe that he'd had the power to cause this brief disruption.

He was reluctant to surrender the delirious rush of power that came over him that day. His mind raced. His little heart pounded. He held the world in his hand and believed that all around him was fluid and subject to his will. But he was a good boy, too, and feared the thought of his mother and siblings trapped forever in this state of unbeing, though he might have left his father like that for all time if he'd been able. He released the pendulum with a delicate push, closed the clock face, and the day jumped back to life.

HE STOOD AT THE edge of the crowd on Rosen-heimerstrasse in the Bavarian capital three weeks after stealing the first detonator and listened to the cheers rising from inside the beer hall. A band of cloud blighted the dying late-afternoon light. Street lamps flickered on. It was the anniversary of the 1923 Munich Putsch during which Hitler had stormed the Bürgerbräukeller with six hundred men and declared, with a pistol shot into the ceiling, that the national revolution had begun. Two days later he was arrested and soon after condemned to Landsberg Prison. Now every year on this day in November the Party gathered to celebrate the birth of the mighty struggle that awaited.

Pretty girls dressed in colourful dirndls walked through the crowd offering beer and sausage cuttings from wooden platters. The event had about it the high spirits of a country fair. Grease and burning tobacco smells hung over the street, and nearby stood a group of schoolgirls, giggling as they tidied their hair and competed for the one compact mirror among them. Elser felt their energy; they were flirtatious, hungry with intention, excited to be party to the occasion, as if waiting for a handsome headmaster who'd dazzle them with his worldliness and restraint.

SA men dressed in sharp uniforms stood at attention on either side of the entrance to the beer hall, their weapons pointed at the ground.

The speeches—piped outdoors by a system of wires and speakers—were of the type Elser was used to hearing on the radio—repetitive, obsequious, and bitter. They told of past injustices and the coming glories of a resurgent and grateful nation. Sleep no more, a voice intoned. Another spoke of a people on the march. They spoke of community and of better times ahead. All of them spoke of the man who would lead them from the servitude of Versailles and the crimes of its reparations and territorial demands.

The passions of the crowd grew, the defiance and delight crackling as if with electricity, and when Hitler's voice finally issued from the loudspeaker there rose a rapturous applause and a round of adoring salutes. As Elser clapped, he noted the precise time as indicated on his wristwatch, and afterwards, too, when the oration finally came to a close, and soon after the entourage emerged from the beer hall.

Cheers and yet more applause rose as the Chancellor walked through the crowd in the direction of the three cars waiting at the curb. He was dwarfed by the men who surrounded him—political chiefs, officers, and bodyguards—but a clear view suddenly opened between him and Elser. The two men locked eyes, and Elser, who'd committed his crime a hundred times over in his mind by now, believed the plot would be written clear as day on his face. The SA men would come for him. It was all over, and barely even begun, all of it vanished like smoke.

But now the Chancellor was holding a bouquet of carnations and speaking with a young girl. He nodded in agreement, smiling, and kissed her forehead, then continued on to the black Mercedes that waited at the curb. Once in the car, he raised the flowers to his nose and seemed to take in their fragrance with a deep, hallucinatory breath.

Elser wondered what killing a man would feel like, or if he'd feel anything at all. He'd be in another city when it happened, if the bomb successfully detonated one year from today. But he wondered if his soul would know and feel the moment somehow, as a flame at a fingertip registers in the brain. He'd been raised in the ways of the Protestant Church. The belief that only faith and good deeds delivered you to the Lap of God was one he could not unlearn. It was seared into him. For this one, sharp moment he wavered.

He entered the banquet hall for the first time an hour later, after the crowd had finally dispersed. It was a grand room cluttered with long tables and overturned benches and ringed by a second-floor balcony that looked down over the wide-open space. The air was still heavy with tobacco smoke and the smell of spilled beer. A team of women swept the floors of pamphlets and stacked beer glasses and plates onto wheeled carts, ignoring him as he studied the position of the speaker's rostrum in front of the pillar that supported the balcony. Wood-panelled from floor to waist height, the brick was covered over with white plaster. One of the washerwomen turned and asked if he'd forgotten something. He shook his head and bent to pick up one of the pamphlets and carried it to the restaurant-tavern that was linked to the banquet hall by a brick passageway.

The waitress there greeted him and led him forward to a table, where he sat and ate a meal of sausage and potato and blue cabbage. On the back of the pamphlet he sketched from memory a drawing of the pillar and the speaker's rostrum and the small stick figure of the man who would stand before it a year from today.

HE WAS FOCUSED NOW. He worked slowly, pacing himself, always careful. He created a false bottom in his lunch box and carried out more detonators from the armaments factory, two or three at a time, only a few of which he'd need to build the seven bomb prototypes he'd later test in the back quarter of his parents' orchard over the coming months.

When he decided he'd taken enough and could steal nothing more of any value, he found a way to get himself fired, and two weeks later he rode a bus up to the Vollmer quarry, eighteen miles north of Königsbronn, and petitioned for a job as a quarryman.

He needed access to dynamite.

Over the two months he worked there he accumulated two hundred and fifty packages of gunpowder, eighty-three blasting caps, and sixty-eight cartridges of Donarit 3. He required only a fraction of this for the prototypes he was already sketching in the notebook he carried with him everywhere. He hid what he stole in the closet in the room he rented from the Schmauder family in Schnaitheim, two miles from the quarry. He left the quarry in May and stayed with his parents in Königsbronn for a month, where three days in a row he churned the earth of his parents' orchard with the bombs he worked on through the night. In August, nine months after he first visited that city, he boarded the train to Munich.

Here he rented a room in the flat of an old couple named Baumann. It was a small space that overlooked an interior courtyard filled with drying laundry, bicycles, and a store of coal piled beneath a rusted-tin lean-to. One evening his landlords found the tools he often laid out on the desk in his room—among them pliers and a soldering iron and a coil of copper wire. These tools were common in his declared trade. He'd told them he was a cabinetmaker and inventor of household appliances that would improve the lives of ordinary people. He knew working people had few enough hours in the day as it was. He smiled as he explained the nature of his inventions-in-progress to Frau Baumann. It was slow going, he said, but surely he would get there. The old lady nodded and clicked her tongue against her teeth in a way that was her habit and told him she couldn't agree more, not enough hours, she said, not enough at all, God as my witness. He paid his weekly rent a day in advance, left no signs of himself anywhere in the flat other than in his room and the shoes he left on the mat to the inside right of the entrance beside the coat rack. They had no problem with their quiet lodger, who worked mostly in his room all day long, leaving the apartment only to buy supplies and to take a late supper at a nearby restaurant from time to time. He seemed busy with industry, of which they approved, a driven individual who might one day better the lot of the common working family with the mysterious inventions he tinkered at into the small hours.

He ate at the Bürgerbräukeller as often as three times a week over his last two months in the city. He kept a mental note of each new face he saw. The intermingling of military with civilian was usual enough in these times. Soldiers were everywhere now. He saw them in the morning when he called in at the shops where he purchased the supplies he needed—copper wire, batteries, paraffin wax—never visiting the same hardware store or electrical supplier more than once. He paid little attention to the Wehrmacht men. They were regular soldiers, not drawn particularly to the cause, he thought—farm boys, machinists, school drop-outs eager for adventure. It was Hitler's bullyboys, the SA men and Gestapo, he feared. When he saw this sort he walked steadily on, nodding perhaps in their direction if they seemed to take an interest in him. He did what he could to control the anxiety that took hold of him at these times. In the evening, when he saw a group of these killers enter through the high double doors of the Bürgerbräu-keller, he always wondered if they were coming for him, his secret discovered, revealed perhaps by a snooping landlady or curious shopkeeper. He attempted to put this fear out of his mind, taking on the appearance of a man simply enjoying his supper, and when his hands began to shake uncontrollably as they neared his table he'd return his knife and fork to his plate and rest his trembling hands on his knees, safely out of sight under the table, where the satchel bearing his tools rested against his leg.

He was always observing, that fall, more alone than he'd ever been as he waited for the next opportunity to slip into the adjacent banquet hall to continue his work. Certain officers, as he waited through October and into November, became familiar to him in their routine and schedule; they came often, as he did, and always the men and women of the neighbourhood arrived—families and bureaucrats and tradesmen; sometimes students flush with Reichsmarks and the wealth of national pride that puffed their chests.

He often sat close enough to hear the creak of the leather of their boots and their belts, from which hung their side-arms. They spoke of the women they had conquered and the cities they soon would and the fortune that awaited a man who knew what he wanted in life. It was usually loud here, and louder still when waiters came and went through the kitchen swing door at the back of the room, industrious staff calling out orders, and the light from cooking fires illuminating the clouds of cigarette smoke that hung in the air. But the banquet hall was quiet on those nights he worked, reserved as it was for special dates in Munich's social calendar and the sort of political gathering he was preparing for. The two large rooms were connected by the short corridor leading off the foyer near the restaurant-tavern's exit, a darkened length of bricked archway that began at one heavy set of dark doors and ended at another, on the other side of which was a deep and unseen quiet.

Always he felt his stomach turn when he walked through the crowd of officers, their faces alight with good cheer and menace and celebration. He'd always been a bad liar. He was terrified that his halting step and the sweat on his brow would give away his treachery. This was the overriding fear that possessed him in the early days of his sabotage. It was the world of surfaces that would betray him. A trembling hand. An eyelid twitching with nerves. A bead of sweat on the brow on a cool September evening.

Once he listened to a man at the table next to his speak of the events in Poland that the press had taken to calling Bloody Sunday. Atrocities against the ethnic German minority in Bydgoszcz had proven beyond a doubt—if there had been any doubt to begin with, the man said—that Germany must continue to demand reparations. "Hundreds of Germans, can you imagine—people like you and me simply trying to live their lives!" He was trembling with rage, this man. The story had affected Elser, too. The photographs published in the *Völkischer Beobachter* showed corpses of women and children dumped in a roadside ditch. He'd felt revulsion and anger when he saw the pictures, as he knew the whole nation would, and understood too well that they'd further stoke populist rage against the Poles.

ON A RAINY EVENING in late October a patron turned to him and said he'd just come down from Freiberg, and was he familiar with that lovely town? This man sold insurance and had been doing business up there in Baden-Württemberg, he said. Elser rarely engaged with the other diners, avoiding conversation when he could. But that evening he was taken up in the grip of nostalgia.

A lovely place, indeed, he said.

He told the man of his trips to the region as a boy with his father in the time before his father turned drunken and violent. This might have been 1909 or 1910. Discarding his usual caution, he carved a dangerous trail into his true past that might be used one day to find him, once he was done here.

He spoke about the stands of white pine that seemed to go on forever. Sometimes he'd walked with his father for an entire morning in complete silence, so entranced by the beauty around them. His father, hailing from deep within another century, country-born with hands like wooden paddles, had tormented his children and wife with an alcoholic tyrant's rage. But out there in those hills the countryside seemed to bring him peace. A vicious old man, otherwise, he told the stranger. But weren't they all like that back then, beaten in their turn, and those before them beaten too, the miserable cycle forever repeated? It was not for the likes of his father that he'd execute this act of grace he'd set himself. On this point he held his tongue. It would come in the name of the meek and the fearful, as he himself had been in his youth, oppressed and powerless under his father's heel.

On one such trip into the hills of the Black Forest, the boy Elser and his father had watched brook trout holding in the stream they'd stopped to drink from. In the heat of the summer's day he'd stripped off his clothes and slipped into the water, scattering the trout. He was for that moment fully and simply happy, he remembered. His father sat back against a tree and opened the rucksack and rooted around in there for the bottle he'd brought, then called the boy over and asked him where it was. The boy stood before him, naked in his shame. He'd thrown the bottle away, he said. His father nodded and rose to his feet and led the boy back to the stream and told him to look at himself in the water's surface, for he was a thief and needed to recognize the wretch that he was. When Georg did as he was told, his father pushed his head into the water and pressed his face hard against the streambed. With the other hand he beat the boy's bare arse until his son broke free and rolled over, gasping for breath.

From that time on the hatred was always there, as were the beatings, and he imagined his father dying by his hand, practising it over and over in his mind. The man beat all of his children, but Georg seemed to be his favourite target, and this all-consuming hatred for despots became the long preparation for the project that awaited him now.

For years afterwards he did nothing when he saw a man beaten in the streets—a labour unionist or Jew or someone who'd spoken out against the regime. He'd turn away in shame, mortified for the direction this new Germany seemed so eager to follow. It could not last much longer. The Social Democrats and the Communists would unite against the National Socialists and a wave of common decency would wash over the country. The madness would end.

But it didn't, and wouldn't, he saw now, until the nation rose in defiance.

He offered his hand to the insurance man at the end of their meal together, tipped his hat, and wished him luck.

ELSER LOOKED FOR OTHER distractions until he was able to slip unseen into the banquet hall. He found it in the kindness of his waitress and the pleasure he took in her smile and her backside, which moved like two Christmas plum cakes beneath her bright dirndl. Despite a nervous stomach, he enjoyed the meals she brought him and the half-mug of beer he allowed himself on these nights. When he paid his bill and thanked her, he wanted to believe she knew about the brave secret in his heart and that she admired him and wished him Godspeed, though he understood this was just one of the many small fantasies he allowed himself. He imagined returning here one day to tell her how he'd watched her these lonely weeks as he moved towards the end of his long project. The war would be over, stopped by him. She would thank him, as the entire nation would, and she'd seat him as the returning hero he was and serve him a meal fit for a king. Without you, she'd say . . .

And then his imagination floundered and it was just him again as he sat waiting for his night's work to begin.

It was a test of his resolve to walk with anything resembling composure through the restaurant while men in uniform spoke in loud voices or weaved drunkenly as they returned from the restroom.

One of these men, a sergeant with a large stomach, pushed his chair out as Elser passed behind him one evening. The chair caught the satchel strung off Elser's shoulder, causing it to fall to the floor. The man laughed and apologized and bent to pick it up. He held it in his hand a moment, as if weighing its contents, then passed it back to him with a backslap and guffaw.

He didn't enter the banquet hall that evening. His courage failed him. He'd never come so close to being found out. For the next three nights he stayed away, wondering if he should abandon the plot.

WHEN HE RESUMED HIS work the following week it seemed nothing had changed. After his meal at the restaurant-tavern he waited for the right moment, then walked down the hallway to the banquet hall and pushed through the heavy doors. Inside it was pitch-black and silent, as it always was. He felt along the walls as he proceeded, the geography of the space learned by touch and the counting of footsteps. He took his place where he always did, in the storeroom, and tried to sleep for an hour or two until it was time to get to work.

He learned to choreograph his labours to the automatic flush of toilets that echoed out from the corridor at the north end of the hall. It came every ten minutes and lasted thirty-three seconds, covering the sound of his intermittent work. The glow of the flashlight he carried in the satchel was softened by the blue rag he tied over its face, casting a melancholy hue over his slow, steady progress.

It took him six nights to construct the panel in the wainscotting that encased the brick pillar. The panel would cover the cavity he dug there, in which he would place his bomb, and be fitted back into place after a night's work, its vertical edges slotted tightly into the existing jointing in the wainscotting. On the sixth night the panel was finished. He examined it closely in the blue light of the beam. It was an invisible perfect fit.

On the seventh night he began carving out the inside of the pillar's brickwork. He chipped away at the mortar one toilet flush at a time, his elation building when a brick was about to give, and finally when it came away he leaned back on his heels and placed the brick in the open satchel beside him. With the successful removal of each new brick he permitted himself a sip of water from his canteen.

At the end of a night's work, often still two hours before first light, he covered the hole with the panel, collected his tools, cleaned and dusted the area, and slipped back into the storeroom. Here he waited for the sound of the adjacent tavern to begin its day's trade before stepping out into the alleyway by the service entrance and turning left onto Kellerstrasse, just another early riser on his way to work. He took various routes back to his room, emptying the satchel of its night's worth of broken brick and mortar, never in the same place twice, and then got himself back to his room to sleep for an hour or two before rising again to continue building the bomb he'd place inside the pillar.

NEARING THE END OF his project, after thirty-one nights in the banquet hall, he worried through the problem of the two metronomes—the timing devices—that required a true surface. The bottom of the chamber inside the pillar was rough and uneven. He'd been unable to purchase a spirit level small enough to fit inside the cavity.

His anxiety grew as Germany pushed deeper into war. There was word of British forces in France now, a hundred thousand or more. Polish access to the Baltic Sea via the Danzig Corridor had been cut. A German U-boat had sunk the British battleship *Royal Oak* at Scapa Flow, in the Orkney Islands. The world was coming apart, and time was wasting for the problem of a spirit level.

One night he watched his waitress as she moved through the crowd between tables, serving tray raised above heads, while he puzzled over this latest challenge. She was an attractive woman, the one whose shapely behind allowed him a moment of fancy in the midst of his work. Unerringly pleasant when she set his meal before him, she called him Georg and asked after his day, though she didn't pry either, or really care, for that matter, he imagined. This was simply a social pleasantry, a welcoming disposition that he appreciated as he sat here doing his calculations.

That's when he saw the man at the next table place a small handful of coins on her tray. The coins rolled in riot and tumbled from the tray to the floor.

He purchased the bag of marbles at the toy shop two

blocks over from the Baumanns' flat the following day, and after the restaurant-tavern closed that night he selected a serving tray from the shelf in the storeroom and placed it at the bottom of the hole he'd created in the brick pillar. The marbles told him where and by how much he must adjust the height of this corner or that, a bit lower, a bit higher, depending on the direction the marbles rolled. He shone his torch on them like a boy at play, knees and back aching, delighted that he'd solved the problem with the help of this simple game.

He set the two timers for nine-twenty the following night, the second a failsafe for the first. They were powered by a zinc electrode battery, the clock movements connected to the detonating caps he'd taken from the Waldenmaier warehouse. Kneeling, torch in hand, he studied his work with satisfaction. He was pleased with its ingenuity and workmanship, and the stealth and cleverness that it represented. The nerves that had assailed him at the beginning of his work here weeks earlier had been quieted. On this last night he was practised, calm, and perfect.

He adjusted his position and lifted the torch's beam away from the bomb and traced it up the back of the support pillar of the low balcony above. It would come down with the blast. He directed the light into the chamber once more and fought the urge to reach in again to check that the battery was live and the timers level and balanced, that its wires were properly connected and the cork soundproofing secured properly against the interior brick. It was after four in the morning, time to move. He'd wait in the storage room until those footsteps arrived, and then make his way to Konstanz, connecting via Ulm and Friedrichshafen. By eleven the following night he'd board the ferry that would deliver him across the lake. There he'd adopt the leisurely stride of a tourist as he moved in the direction of the park at the Wessenbergheim, where he'd find the border crossing into Switzerland.

Setting in place the access panel for the last time, he felt it snap into position. He collected his tools and dusted away the loose debris—crumbs of brick and the clippings of wire casing, like a razed colony of black ants. With his handkerchief he polished the panel and the stone floor. Everything was clean and ready again for the coming day. He stood and arched backwards to correct for the difficult posture he'd held for too long, knees burning, then stepped away and moved the beam of light over the door and the base of the pillar. He saw nothing that didn't belong, nothing that would be noticed. At last satisfied, he carried the satchel and suitcase to the storeroom and quietly shut the door.

He cleared his head of the business at hand and invoked some distracting memory. It was no use. Tonight sleep would not come. He visualized the plan as he'd constructed it; only steps away, where the orators would address the gathering, the clock movements steadily ticked down. He'd be long gone by the time the hall filled. But he was tempted now to stay in the city to watch events unfold. Here would be witnessed the beginnings of a new life for the country, and from this point on he would be the father of a new Germany. The anxiety ran through him again as it had in the early days of this work. It was too early to dream of a new era. Nothing was sure. There were still too many points at which his intricate plan might fail. He feared that the serving tray— the base on which the contraption sat—might have shifted under a pebble of mortar that he might have missed. A true and even foundation was crucial. He fought the urge to check it again as he sat there in the dark storeroom. Finally, nearing six-thirty, the sound of the first employee entering the adjacent room caught his ear. Soon after that the man entered the hall and unlocked the rear door through which Elser slipped moments later.

It was still cold and dark out but he felt the elation of freedom take hold. He was almost done. Now, just to leave. The concern he'd felt over the timing device burned away in the promise of daylight. He filled his lungs, and half a block on when he turned the corner he tipped his hat and smiled at an old woman peeling potatoes she took from a basket as she sat on a front step.

He enjoyed two cups of coffee in Isartorplatz and afterwards made for the train station. He bought his ticket and stood waiting on the platform among the crowd of travellers, his suitcase already packed and at his side. He was prepared, everything was in place. Nazi banners and flags over the street flapped in the wind. The day looked like any other. A stiff breeze blew from the north, causing men to grip the hats on their heads. Businesses carried on, motor vehicles and bicycles and trams clattered, and the movement of the timing wheel housed in the hollowed-out pillar at the beer hall marched down to the moment that would usher in a new Republic.

HE WAS ALREADY MORE than a hundred miles west of Munich when the bomb spread its chaos and shards of brick and mortar through the banquet hall. He heard nothing that announced the arrival of a new era, of course—no explosion, no heralding trumpet blast, no hallelujahs—only the soothing clatter of the train that carried him. It was odd, though, the shift he felt in the coach compartment at that instant. The man seated opposite him seemed to notice it too. He raised his eyes from his reading and stared at Elser with a curious look on his face, as if at that moment the stranger sitting across from him became a different man from the one who'd sat there since boarding two hours earlier. When the lights of the Meersburg Bahnhof finally appeared, Elser felt but could not be certain that the culmination of his year-long project had been a success.

Once detrained, he passed through the echoing halls of the Bahnhof and hailed a cab that would deliver him to the ferry terminal two miles distant. There he purchased his ticket for the crossing and waited in a dockside tavern for the boat to put in.

At a table for two he sat alone and warmed his hands on a pot of tea and watched the snow begin to fall outside the window. From here he could see men at the foot of the pier with their ropes and lanterns beating their arms against the cold as they prepared to bring the ferry in. Most of the patrons in the tavern were waiting for the crossing, though a few locals, drawn perhaps by habit and not travel, huddled with their mugs of beer by the fire that crackled in the hearth set in a stone wall hung with hunting trophies. Voices around the room were desultory and muted, a deep contrast to the riot that sounded in Elser's head. He felt the terrible unease of not knowing what had happened, if the timers had stalled out or a detonating fuse had burned down to nothing. These were distinct possibilities. Word should have come by now. He wondered if he shouldn't return to the city to see the job through. It was an agonizing interlude, the fire and hope that had risen in him while on the train dimming darker by the minute as he sat waiting.

When the telephone at the bar rang, he watched the bartender pick it up and talk and listen, the expression on the man's face changing slowly from one of confusion to disbelief to alarm. His brow darkened, and as he finally returned the receiver to its cradle, Elser understood that news of the events he'd been waiting to hear about had finally arrived.

The man came around from the bar and pulled the waitress

aside and spoke into her ear. She was a small, unhappy-looking woman of perhaps thirty who might have felt more at ease on a milking stool than she did tending to travellers at this lakeside tavern. She covered her mouth with the back of her hand when he spoke to her, then leaned heavily against a nearby table, as if these whispers had delivered a crippling blow.

The man reading a book at a corner table looked up. He watched the woman for a moment before rising from his seat to ask if he could be of assistance. He was a doctor, he said. As word of the events in Munich spread, the sullen mood that had presided over the tavern grew animated. Debate regarding the merits of the rumour intensified and continued when the boarding call came. The room emptied. Travellers made their way in small groups across the road to the slip and slowly came aboard. In the passageways, on the upper decks, and in the lounge people huddled in conference. When the ferry put in at Konstanz forty-five minutes later, past eleven o'clock, the snow was heavier now as Elser disembarked and made his way up from the harbour into the village in the direction of the Swiss border. It drifted on currents of air in the glow of the street lamps lining Schiffstrasse.

In the light of a sandwich-shop window he stopped and watched three men listening to the radio placed between them on a table. Word was spreading. His work had been of some consequence, at least; his labours had shaken the country. He couldn't know the final measure of his efforts yet, but he'd shown that it was possible to get this close to the heart of the monster. Even if the top leadership had not been killed, this action would inspire others; the people would rise and finally return the government to the Republic.

He found a crowd collecting in the main square, drawn into their small cheerless groups by the wireless updates that were coming in every few minutes now. An act of villainy had been perpetrated in the Bavarian capital, the bulletins stated, and its full consequences were still unknown. The nation was awaiting further information. Sorrow and disbelief and stifled sobs filled the snowy square. He didn't stop to listen for details, eager though he was for confirmation. Instead he continued west out of town up into the foothills where, ten minutes later, he saw the crossing gate that was the border.

He didn't alter his pace when the man, cigarette in hand, emerged from the guardhouse set off to the side of the road. He'd been rehearsing this moment for weeks, the name Feuchtelhuber ready on his lips—the friend he was visiting on the other side of the border, he'd say, in the next town just up the hill. The guards would see an ordinary traveller, perhaps, or a restless insomniac prone to walking the lonely hills at night.

The simplicity of the lie emboldened him. He ran through it one last time, like a magician rehearsing his deception moments before meeting his audience. He was not a threat, after all—not anymore—so he waved and called a greeting to the guard from twenty paces and opened his coat to show that he had nothing to hide. As he approached he saw the second man seated in the guardhouse and heard the strains of music coming faintly through the night. The man stepped out to join his colleague as the music grew louder. It was a song by Schubert that his mother had often sung to him while he drifted to sleep. He handed his papers to the first man.

The falling snow caught the light of the guardhouse and shimmered like silver waves against the night. Elser attempted to appear at ease, imagining himself safely on the other side of that crossing gate, seated perhaps in a comfortable hotel lounge contemplating the news of the events he'd set in motion, his part in all this now settled.

A sombre voice interrupted the music on the radio and announced the death in Munich of the heart and soul of the nation. Treachery had cast its dark shadow over the land, the voice said. A villainous Bolshevik conspiracy had shaken the nation and would be crushed. Border crossings were being closed, all suspicious travellers detained.

The guards unholstered their sidearms and questioned this man, so oddly wandering the countryside at this late hour. They examined his papers again, more closely, and searched him, and asked the nature of his business at this time of night. He told them his lies, so calmly rehearsed as he'd walked this road, but now they came jumbled and confused, and the fear that rose in him brought more questions and caused the guards to believe that this was a man with secrets.

THE FOLLOWING DAY THEY returned him to Munich where he was held in Stadelheim Prison at the edge of consciousness for two months while they taught him that everything he knew about pain and longing and willpower had been until that time nothing but the imaginings of a coddled child. The relief in knowing that he'd released Germany from its doomed history lasted only days. He'd created a moment that would be seized upon, he thought. A coup would follow. The fanaticism that had gripped the country would be crushed. It was still reasonable to believe this twelve hours into his detention, despite the beating he received when he arrived at the prison—even thirty-six hours later he was able to believe it. It was an expectation that buoyed him as he waited those first nights for the men to come and pull him from his cell to resume the interrogation. He imagined, instead of beatings, the triumphant news that the coup had begun—people were rising in the streets, they'd say, soldiers deserting their posts. Surely it had begun. His act of defiance would create opportunity to be seized upon. Moderates would be emboldened; the people would move against what was left of the regime. The men who came to his cell door would raise him on their shoulders and present him as a hero of the nation. But they did not come.

He was raised on no one's shoulders.

Instead, he was taken from his cell and strung naked by his ankles from a beam in a cold room in which paced the head of the Reichskriminalpolizeiamt. This man's name was

Arthur Nebe. He was a compact, smiling man who nodded his head with pleasure when his assistant enacted the various tortures Nebe was fond of dreaming up.

Over the first nine days and nights of the interrogations Elser learned nothing of the chain of events he'd set in motion. On the eleventh day Nebe told him the American Republican presidential nominee, Joseph Kennedy, had attended Hitler's funeral in Berlin, just three days earlier. It had been a solemn and beautiful occasion, he said, during which Kennedy had spoken of his great respect for the fallen leader. The next day the American politician attended the ceremony that saw Göring elevated to the Chancellery. He joined him later that afternoon on the Reichstag balcony and spoke to the assembled masses of the sitting President Roosevelt's foolish lust for war in Europe, which the Republican nominee would avoid at all costs should he win the presidential election twelve months from now.

Elser watched the man's face in disorienting glimpses as he spun in slow circles.

"We do not speak of this openly, of course," Nebe said, "but the nation will thank you one day. The Austrian Gypsy understood only zealotry and fear. And we all know zealots do not win wars. Göring, though. Yes. A man who understands military strategy and tactics. You have cleared the way. We should come to you bearing flowers for the service you've done your country. Instead of this." He raised his hand and gestured to the pathetic sight before him. "Such a pity we cannot pay the hero-assassin his proper due."

THERE WAS LITTLE IN his background to suggest Elser possessed the talents required to execute this plot unaided. A trade unionist and small-time communist, a little man, he was too ordinary for anyone to believe that he'd carried out so complex an operation on his own. This Mr. Feuchtelhuber, Nebe said—the name he'd offered the guards at the Swiss border—had been waiting to guide him through to a safe house where he would continue this conspiracy with the men who controlled him, wasn't that right? A second explosion had gone off in the city the very day of the assassination. The work of British agents, Nebe said, who now enjoyed the same treatment as Elser in this very prison. The wider web of lies was waiting to be discovered, he assured him. They would need names before they finally hanged him, and until then he would be kept alive. He told Nebe and the others who interrogated him that the name he'd offered the guards at the border had been an invention. They had him repeat every step of his plan over and over. Days in a row they asked the same questions. When he wasn't suspended by a rope or tied to a chair they had him sketch the floor plan of the banquet hall and the schematics of the bomb he'd perfected. He told them about his regular meals at the Bürgerbräukeller and timing his work to coincide with the sound of the automatic flushing of toilets. He told them about his love for his country and his desire to save Germany from the disaster that was coming.

ON THE TWELFTH DAY of his detention they cleaned him up, fed him, and brought him to an office with a window overlooking a prison courtyard. Nebe stood with him at the window and watched a man wearing a cotton-sack prisoner's uniform push a wooden handcart across the gravel yard. Overhead the sky was grey. Three guards trailed behind the man, one smoking a cigarette. The prisoner set down the handles of the cart at the foot of the scaffolding that dominated the square and waited for the guards. The one who'd been smoking tossed his cigarette and produced a length of rope from his coat and bound the hands of the condemned man. The two others walked the prisoner up the steps and positioned him on the trap door. They placed a cloth sack over his head and fastened the noose around his neck and stepped away. The prisoner rolled his head and raised his chin, as a man does after securing a fresh Windsor knot, attempting to find the right fit. The trap door opened. The prisoner dropped and bounced at the end of the rope.

"Some of them, it takes more than once," Nebe said.

He handed Elser a pencil and a pad of paper and had him draw yet another diagram of his bomb. With the three fingers that remained unbroken on his right hand he produced the drawing, and one of the timing device; he wrote the name of the factory in Königsbronn where he'd worked and the addresses of the locations where he'd purchased the materials he'd used and the name of the old couple he'd rented his room from. Later that day he was provided a workshop where he was to construct a facsimile of the bomb using items similar to the ones he'd taken from the armaments factory and the materials he'd purchased in Munich. They wanted to see if he was capable of doing the things he claimed he'd done.

His torturers admired the intricacy of the plan. Privately, they began to believe he'd worked alone. His ingenuity impressed Nebe. In a flash of delirium Elser almost believed they'd let him go for the respect he'd earned. Every day he asked them to kill him, but they would not grant this simple favour. Nebe was expert at bringing a man's soul to the surface and keeping it there, beating and alive for hours, before letting it slip back into darkness.

ON THE FIFTEENTH DAY of his torture he was led into a room in which he heard the sounds of a woman sobbing. He listened through the cloth sack covering his head, his heart already ripped with fear. It was not the usual screams and cries of pain that haunted the prison at all hours. These sounds were soft and familiar, almost comforting to hear. He stood on uncertain legs, his body and spirit weakened by beatings and exhaustion and thirst, hands cuffed behind his back. And then he understood what this was. He knew before the hood was removed.

He turned his face away so his mother would not see what they'd done to him, but a hand took a fistful of hair at the back of his head and pulled him straight to give his mother a good look at her half-dead son. She was seated at a small table beside his sister, Maria, delivered here to witness this torture. He attempted to nod his head to tell them he could feel nothing now. They should not fear for him. It would be a final comforting lie. He wanted to tell them that what he'd done he'd done for them and every other German. They could be proud of him and know that he'd accept his death a thousand times over for the bloodshed he'd helped prevent. He wanted to say all this with a look or a nod of his head, but they saw nothing of the sort, only the terrified eyes of a son and a brother.

His torturers had not brought Elser's family there that day to watch his interrogations, though. What Nebe needed now was for Elser to watch the torture of those he loved. When he understood this, he pleaded and told him he would say anything. He would confess to any sort of foreign conspiracy they wished, a Jewish one, or communist, whatever they needed from him. And when it began and did not stop, he begged for their forgiveness, and that was the last time he saw his people.

IN JANUARY, TWO MONTHS after his capture, he was delivered to Wiesbaden and put on a barge that would carry him and sixty other men to one of the Rhine Meadow labour camps, where they'd be worked until they died. He watched the hill towns and vineyards on the riverbank as the barge moved north and wondered in his delirium if he wasn't already dead. He knew little about the specifics of the place he was going to, or the leadership of the country as it had reshaped itself after the death of Hitler. His imprisonment had kept him in a state of unknowing, but for scraps of news Arthur Nebe had thrown him. The landscape slipped under a blanket of cloud, and rain began to fall as the barge cut north, down-river, with its cargo of men and fear and drowned hope.

THE CAMP WAS A city of earthworks and wooden shacks built at the bottom of the deep valley they called the Devil's Cup. It was encircled by tiers of barbed wire and eighteen guard towers positioned at quarter-mile intervals along the ridge of the valley. Within an hour of his arrival Elser witnessed a guard beating a man to death for the crime of shivering in his presence. The man, shrunken by starvation, received these blows with hands braced about the back of his head. Within days the beatings he witnessed no longer moved him. He learned the necessity of minding one's own business. Yet sometimes he could not help but watch what played out before him. He saw one man kill another in a dispute over a heel of bread. He saw men die of starvation, of typhus and cholera and gangrene and the tireless parasites that haunted the lung or bowel or liver. They died of smallpox and diphtheria. Many were shot or beaten or froze to death that winter and were replaced, and the new prisoners were put to work in the nearby factories, mines, and fields until they themselves died. The Devil's Cup was mud most of the year until the winter turned the mud into a rock-solid surface that split your head when a guard slammed you to the ground. The groups of men within each barrack kept mostly to themselves, groups of twenty, but these groups were constantly changing as men perished, some in their sleep—a whisper of mercy, perhaps, in repayment for some long-forgotten virtue. Twice in the span of seven days he awoke beside a man who'd been so blessed, and by nightfall there was another man in that bunk to take his place.

In those first months, in the early winter of 1940, he looked for signs that the war of aggression had slowed, and that Germany would soon sue for a negotiated peace. But instead came talk of an escalation in the war and the string of successes enjoyed by the new Chancellor. The German divisions that rolled through Western Europe to the edge of the English Channel were well supplied and buoyed by victory, the rumours said. The massacre at Bydgoszcz avenged now, Poland had been crushed and divided, all territories west of the Molotov-Ribbentrop Line falling under German control. The Soviets, by agreement, held the east. Speculation abounded that Göring himself would stroll the beach at Calais before summer came, and from there he'd witness smoke rising over the Channel as London burned. Poor weather had stalled the German advance through the Scandinavian countries. But soon the spring thaw would come to permit land access all the way to the Barents Sea.

When word arrived in late November of the upset victory in the American elections, Elser took the news as a man does his own imminent death. President Roosevelt, weakened by polio, had fallen ill in the last months of the campaign. Joseph Kennedy, former ambassador to the United Kingdom turned Republican challenger, had promised peace for America and peace it would have. The catastrophe that would be American involvement in the war in Europe was all but certain if Roosevelt managed to clinch a third term, he argued. His promise had been rewarded with a landslide. Kennedy's running mate, Strom Thurmond, set out on a victory tour of America with the aviation hero Charles Lindbergh, leader of the America First Committee, while the president-elect crossed the Atlantic to personally assure Berlin that he was a man of his word.

In April of 1941 the Bavarian typesetter who replaced the second man to die in the cot next to Elser's told of the non-aggression pact that had been signed with America. He also spoke of the Japanese sneak-attack on the Soviet Pacific fleet anchored at Vladivostok, in the Far East. The raid had sent three-quarters of the fleet to the bottom of the harbour. The Red Army was moving east to come to the aid of the besieged city and to meet the expected land invasion there and in the border regions of Mongolia, where Japanese

Imperial forces had been building their presence since 1933. The typesetter had worked at the *Völkischer Beobachter* in Munich, the paper Elser had bought on the morning he read about the Bloody Sunday massacre in Bydgoszcz. His hands were still ink-stained, so swiftly carried out was the sentence that had condemned him. He'd manipulated a story concerning the neutrality of Holland, second only to Portugal as the busiest transit point for refugees waiting to leave Europe. It was a simple enough piece, a story intended to be about the largesse of the German state—there were no barriers for those whose papers were in order. The typesetter could not resist. For months he'd been altering the officially sanctioned copy that was provided for him, leaving off an adjective here, a qualifying phrase there. This time he'd been too ambitious, perhaps, he told Elser, typesetting the words *freies Land* to replace *neutrales Land*, and so declaring to the German readership, if but for one evening edition, that Holland would decide its own politics.

Here was a like-minded soul, Elser thought, a selfless man willing to risk his life for the cause. The following day he decided to tell the typesetter that he was not alone here, he was in the company of the "*bierkeller* bomber." They would find strength in each other's example. The sense of hope that had abandoned him rose again. At roll call he looked for the man among those from their barracks on the mud flats between their flimsy shacks and stood at attention as the evening's speeches and the "Deutschlandlied" were piped through the loudspeaker. He did not see him. Afterwards, he found a new man had taken the typesetter's place in the cot next to his.

He had been shot to death when he failed to heed a warning to step away from the barbed-wire fence, another inmate told him that night. The man who said this was wearing the typesetter's boots. He'd helped lift him into the wagon that made its rounds through the Devil's Cup all day, pulled by two old mares and driven by a Hungarian violinist who played for the camp's officers by night.

IN THE SPRING OF his third year there a new round of typhus ripped through the camp. He was placed in the work gang that managed the cremations in open country west of the valley. They wore rags over their faces, but the rags were threadbare and did not mask the smell of death. They soaked them in the gasoline they were supplied for their labours, but the fumes threatened to overtake them, and so they soaked the rags in their urine. Always there were more bodies waiting. The wagon masters drove their horses until the animals collapsed on their way up the valley roads, and fresh animals were harnessed to the wagons, and again the wagons moved in an endless carrying away of the dead. But always more men arrived by rail and road and river barge, from Poland and Czechoslovakia and the German cities, too—all being emptied now of Bolsheviks and degenerates and Jews; the Romany and the Reds; the disobedient, the headstrong, the suicidal, the crippled, and the mad.

In the half-light of a cool spring morning the first blades of grass emerging from the cracked earth near the ash pits caused him to fall to his knees and weep, until a boot laid him out and stepped on his neck and the guard asked if he wanted to work or to burn. He rose to his feet, and the line of horse-drawn wagons appeared again, and he set to unloading and placing bodies on the pyre. He did this until daylight began to fail and finally a guard called out that their work was done, and they began the long walk back in the direction of the camp.

At a turn in the road Elser motioned that he needed to relieve himself, and the guard waved him off. He stepped down into a shallow gully and dropped his pants. He squatted there as the column of men and guards walked on in the direction of the camp and the machine gun towers looking over the valley below.

With no guard in sight now, he inched his way farther down the incline and waited, as good as dead, and stared at the faltering sky and shivered and clutched himself, and slowly the dark gathered and the quarter moon moved in and out of drifting cloud that drew shadow-shapes over his haunted eyes.

When he got to his feet hours later he saw the guard towers on the valley ridge shining their searchlights in slow, roving arcs down into the valley and turning outwards to the fields beyond the wire in the direction of the cremation pits. There would be patrols and dogs, but there was no sign of these now. By next roll call, they would surely know he was gone.

He walked in a painful crouch in the direction of the dying blooms of light that hovered over the open pits, the smell of burnt flesh and bone and spilled petrol filling the night. He felt the heat from the cremations radiating up from the earth and slowed his pace to warm himself, like a man savouring the last comfort he'd ever know, and when he found the edge of the forest soon after, still leafless in the early spring and dangerously open to a revealing moon, he was absorbed into its cold wooded maze.

HE FOUND WHAT HE was looking for after an hour's walk. The building was dark and silent and set against a cluster of birch trees. He stood at the edge of the forest and waited, breathing heavily now for the pain in his limbs and bloody feet. He listened and watched for a light to turn on or a twig to snap in the woods behind him. There was nothing. No movement, no sound. He moved forward down the lane until three men, sitting in the middle of the compound between the farmhouse and the barn, came into view.

The men didn't seem to have any interest in him. They didn't look up as he approached or seem to care at all that a figure prowled at the edge of their silent meeting. One of them held an arm skyward, the arm and hand perfectly still, as if pointing to some distant planet. He wondered if the typhoid hallucinations that had taken the camp weren't upon him now. He knew the symptoms, had seen them a thousand times over.

The men didn't flinch when he stepped forward, closer still, and now he saw they were not men at all but empty old coats and hats hung on a single shovel-plough and wheat seeder, the trick of some child's game or a gargoyle constructed to ward off nighttime visitors.

He removed the field coat from the shovel-plough and put it on. He checked its pockets and found a box of match-sticks, a cork, and a heel of bread. He broke a piece off and returned the rest to the pocket. It was hard and smelled like leather but he ate it hungrily, swallowing down its dryness with great effort.

He walked to the far side of the compound and placed his ear to the slab-wood barn door. The wood was cold and rough against the side of his face. He listened and eased it back and peered through the dark and saw the animal, head lifted, already staring at him.

She watched as he entered.

He spoke softly, leading with his voice as he studied her, the broad haunches of the animal shifting, the head rolling towards and away from him.

"There you are," he said in a whisper. "Yes, you'll do just fine."

He unlatched the swing gate of her enclosure and waited before entering, speaking in a calm, tuneless voice, and then pulled the gate open and stepped forward and slowly raised his hand to touch her muzzle.

She allowed him to run his hand down the hard bone of her face. He leaned in close for her warmth, placing his neck on hers, and when he finally knew he'd gained her trust he stepped away and located the bridle hanging from a spike on the heavy beam to the inside right of the swing gate. He removed the halter from the animal's head and coaxed her mouth open with his thumb for her to receive the bit. He eased the bridle over her ears and head and pulled her fore-lock out from the leather browband and ran his left hand down along her face again.

When he was done he led the animal from the barn into the compound, past the gargoyle tableau, and up he slid onto the mare's back. He kicked her into a trot and out they rode in the direction of the Rhine.

HE CAME ACROSS THE checkpoint before dawn. Ahead in the darkness were soldiers with carbines slung over their shoulders, cigarette embers aglow. He wondered if this wasn't another illusion of the type he'd seen in the compound. There was a booth off to the side of the road, and in it a man sat reading under the green light of a desk lamp.

He drove the mare a hundred yards into the field and around the checkpoint in a wide semicircle that added time to his journey but finally returned him to the road he'd meant to gain. He travelled on until he saw the first moments of dawn breaking in the east, and he heard the river sounding its slow, deep call through the line of hedge in the distance.

He drew the horse to a stop and slid down and walked her on until the river and the bridge, with its five spans over the water, came into view. For two weeks he'd laboured here, setting down the ties and rail along this stretch of line, before the typhus rolled through camp. He'd counted the skiffs and coal barges and the frequency of their passing as they cut their way north. Now he heard only the broad presence of the river and the blood pulsing in his ears and that call inside his head that told him he would die soon if he didn't leave this place.

He unharnessed the mare, slung the horse tackle over his shoulder, and smacked her on the backside. He studied the intricate iron latticework of the bridge in the grey light. The horizon was brightening now. There was no guardhouse or sentry on the bridge that he could see as he began along the towpath, which in a hundred yards rose in a gradual incline to meet the gravel bed of the rail line.

He walked tie by tie onto the bridge until, midway over the river, he stopped and looked to the opposite bank, still grainy in the half-light, and up the long length of current. He descended on the metal rungs into the open space beneath the track where light streamed through the angles of grille-work as in a church of stained-glass windows. Below him the current moved slowly, the surface turning in small eddies that swelled and flattened again and reappeared. He lay forward on his chest and secured the leather strap unloosed from the horse tackle to the girder at his feet. He bound the double hitch, pulling downwards, testing it where his weight would fall. He would remove the knotted rein from the girder if men came. With a double hitch he could do this with a single pull and retreat unseen into the latticework to wait. Once the knot was tied, he righted himself and wrapped the other end of the leather strap around his fist three times until the blood pounded in his fingers and the fingers began to lose all feeling. He unwrapped it and relaxed the grip, exercising the hand to allow the circulation to return.

At first he didn't hear the approach of the barge as it emerged from the bend a quarter mile distant. It was as if an island of earth had dislodged itself from the bank and now floated towards him. It came fully into view in stages, plugging downriver, its coal cargo still only a grey-black smudge over the water. As he reached for the leather strap, he heard the first footsteps at the far end of the bridge, then the sound of a cough and a man clearing his throat.

In a moment he saw their black boots above his head. The grey of their coats flashed through the latticing and the ties and rail. He'd learned the schedule and faces of the Schutzpolizei who'd crossed on patrol every morning and throughout the day while he'd driven those spikes and watched the river traffic below. They were earlier today than usual, come down from the village whose lights had just now begun to shine against the muted landscape, and there was no time to remove the leather strap he'd secured to the girder. One of the men stopped and leaned forward into the railing half a bridge span from where Elser crouched.

He saw him clearly now, up and to his right, coat flaps opened wide as he urinated into the river, holstered sidearm strapped to the heavy leather belt at his hip, and the grey shako on the man's head with its plume tilted against the rising light. He heard the urine hitting the water far below and the phlegmy cough, and he receded deeper into the ironwork and waited for the footsteps to move off.

He wondered if the other man wasn't pissing into the river from some other point, or leaning out to check the ironwork beneath the bridge to make sure all was clear. He couldn't know this wasn't part of a game of Cat and Mouse his captors might be playing with him, but he gripped the rein below the knot and descended the length of the leather as the barge passed under the bridge's centre span. He hung there a moment, then dropped twenty feet and hit the coal bed at an angle that threw him down against the futtock to portside. The force of the impact loosened a slide of coal that half-buried him, turned on his side, like a ship scuttled in the shallows.

FOR HOURS HE WATCHED the bank slip by as the barge sailed downriver.

Mostly he saw trees and bush and rolling hills, but in the late afternoon of that first day he understood there was another camp out there, set far enough back from the river that he saw no sign of it but not so far as to hide the smell of burning corpses.

Soon after, a church spire and a smattering of stone buildings came into view. Behind these a vineyard rose on a yellow and grey hillside crested by a medieval castle whose slate turrets glinted in the dull afternoon light.

He'd moved as little as possible, still too aware of the pilot in the wheelhouse at the stern who might have seen him drop but had not come down to kick about in the coal looking for what might be a stowaway or simply a trick of the light. Yet the rare beauty of the hillside and the castle had so moved him that he shifted his head and body and watched the view for as long as he could before it disappeared upriver.

A three-span bridge lit by torchlight appeared from the darkness just before midnight. At first he didn't understand what he was looking at when the silhouettes began to assemble —a line of two-headed beasts waiting on the parapet, the glow of the torches behind them as soldiers blew into cupped hands—but then he saw these were people roped together two by two, and as the barge passed under the centre span, they were pushed over the edge and fell and sank below the surface.

The violent shivering and fever were well upon him now. He closed his eyes and dreamed that the body he stood over in the cremation pit was his own. He watched the flames crawl up his arms and said, "There but for the grace of God," and the sky swirled and darkened and cast angel and demon shapes before his eyes.

THE EVENING SUN WAS low in the sky when he came to. He didn't know where he was or how many days had passed. He was thirsty now, more than he'd ever been. A small triangle of rainwater had gathered in the fold of the left arm of his coat. It hovered inches from his mouth. For hours he waited like this without moving, staring at the small puddle, his mouth afire with thirst, for fear that he'd cause the coal to shift and draw the river pilot's notice. He waited for dark before he drank, and when he did he held the small mouthful of water on his tongue until it disappeared, like rain into parched soil.

IT WAS THIRST THAT finally lifted and rolled him over the rail into the water the following day, and fear that made him float face up without moving as he watched the length of the barge slip past. The pilot standing at the helm came into view. He watched Elser for a moment, as if to determine that this was a man and not a dead body, then raised a pistol and sighted Elser along its length. He would remember this as he lay on the stone floor of the Parish Church on the outskirts of London four months later—that in this moment the world in its finality turned serene, as if with the acceptance of death came the understanding that it was his fear of life and not death that bound him in doubt. But the pilot lowered the weapon, watched him a moment longer, and returned to his position in the wheelhouse.

THAT AFTERNOON HE SLEPT in a tumbledown structure, and at dusk he found eggs still warm from their laying in a coop behind a barn over the next hill. Fifty yards on was a timber-frame farmhouse with a thatched roof and a gaunt cow roped to a stake out front. He ate two of the eggs as he watched the house, drinking them from their cracked shells. He placed the three eggs that remained in his coat pocket, warmed his hands with his breath, and waited for the chickens to settle again. The coop was constructed with heavy posts and freshly cut planks, its ceiling so low that it brushed the crown of his head if he stood straight. In a moment the chickens were quiet again. He took one from its roosting perch and broke its neck. Then he stripped it of its feathers and quietly opened it against the end of a nail driven into a mooring post. He sat in the hay and ate the heart and liver, and soon after he left the coop and hid in the woods until it was dark enough again to travel.

IN THE FOLLOWING DAYS he avoided villages and cut through fields and meadows and thick stands of beech and oak, the river always to his right. He never travelled in day-time. By day he slept in clumps of trees and abandoned buildings and once under a bridge that spanned the river that was his guide. He knew where he was now. Railway crossings were marked, which made him understand that the war had not yet come to Germany.

In an old shed one morning he found a pair of boots sturdier than his own and a month-old copy of *Der Stürmer*. He slipped his feet into the newer boots, then settled against the clapboard wall and studied the paper.

On the whole it was little more than propaganda, the pages stained and difficult to read, oil-soaked and torn. But he devoured the news about the Yalta Conference and the meeting between Chancellor Göring and President Kennedy like a starving man. He scanned down to the words *Bewunderung* and *Jüdische Verschwörung* and read that the American president spoke of his admiration for this brave nation that dared to take a stand against the international Jewish conspiracy. With this renewal of the non-aggression pact between the two nations, Kennedy said, the United States would applaud the German people's heroic efforts to return their country to the German people, as America itself would return to the first principles that had shaped its history.

He carried the paper with him for days, hoping to see that he'd misunderstood it when he returned to read it again the following morning. But the report did not change. Göring had stayed the course Hitler had set.

ON THE WINDLESS SIDE of a stack of sweet-smelling birch one evening, when he attempted to conjure in his mind's eye the lost Eden of his childhood, he knew this was only an attempt to save himself from the nightmare he was living. There was no lost Eden, only hard and unforgiving reminders that life was to be endured, your spirit thrashed, hardships borne. The future too was now a dying hope, at the very best a vast uncertainty into which he'd be drawn deeper and deeper. This endeavour to restore order to the world had only plunged the dagger with more violence into the heart of the nation, and now the world was coming apart. He felt the need to ask forgiveness. In that grandfather clock's pendulum he'd held in his hand years earlier, when he'd frozen time with a boy's sense of mischief and wonder, he'd glimpsed the powers of hope and mercy and vengeance, and now he yearned only to return to that moment so that he might undo what he'd done. Doubt plagued him. The idealism that had propelled him into this new world had disappeared brutally, removed from his life like the warmth of a blanket taken from a sleeping child, and here all that remained was the cold, damp evening of his failure.

IN JUNE THE RIVER carried him in the dark over the border into neutral Holland and on into the final leg of his journey to Rotterdam. He spent the first night in a shunted boxcar at the edge of the city. Next morning he set out again along the river by foot, and in the portlands, after half a day's walk, he found a dry-docked beam trawler that became his home for the next six weeks while he took handouts on street corners and opposite the Pilgrim Fathers' Church, where on his third day in the city he learned to kneel to collect his miserable alms.

A week passed before he discovered the location of the British Consular Office. Once he did, he took to leaning against the red brick of the Lumière Cinema across the street, on Rochussenstraat, and watching the visa applicants come and go. Only days before he died, the Bavarian typesetter had told him what he needed to know—that the Dutch had no motivation to restrict the movement of refugees. The problem was on the British end, he'd said. No refugee was allowed to sail without that visa.

He attempted anonymity as he loitered, and when his feet began to trouble him he retreated to a table at the coffee house five doors down where he could observe the consulate. He counted more than a hundred petitioners on his first day alone and wondered who of them had received what they'd come for. There was no one he resembled closely enough to pull off what he'd planned. On a number of occasions he abandoned his vigil and walked through the port, studying the cargo ships and steamers docked there. He learned their schedules and boarding rituals. A week earlier the *Empress of Asia* had sailed for Edinburgh carrying three hundred passengers. Nine days before that the *Pharaon* had embarked for Cardiff. It was not possible to board without the papers he needed. From the far side of the cordoned zone he studied the inspection process as a queue of hundreds of passengers was boarded. Occasionally he saw a man near his own age, of similar weight and height and hair colour, emerge from the Consular Office wearing a smile that, to Elser's mind, suggested his United Kingdom entry permit had been approved. There was no way of knowing, of course, but in any case the similarities, again, were never close enough for him to engage his plan.

THE DAY HE'D BEEN waiting for came in early August when he saw a man, similar in stature to himself, emerge from the consulate. He'd not seen him enter—he'd arrived late that morning—but now the similarities they shared were clear. With dark eyes and hair and dimpled chin, they were also roughly the same age and height and weight.

He followed the stranger down the road, where, five blocks on, the man purchased a clutch of geraniums from a curbside flower-seller. He carried them to the same church where Elser often collected alms.

At the entrance of Pilgrim Fathers' Church, he watched the man place the geraniums at the foot of the Madonna and make the sign of the cross, then seat himself in a pew. The hem of the man's jacket touched the floor when he knelt to pray. Elser entered, crossing himself as he did so, and took a seat behind him. The concentration the stranger gave to his prayer seemed to consume him completely, and Elser wondered if he'd ever know the purity of faith that this man seemed to possess.

He reached forward now, watching the back of the stranger's head, and removed the documents and wallet from the open side pocket. And then he rose to his feet, crossed himself, and exited the church.

RENTING A ROOM WAS the first test. The man's eyes in the photograph he'd stolen were not down-turned, as Elser's were. He could do nothing about that, or the wider mouth, but the full black hair and eyebrows were similar, as were the nose and cheekbones. The concierge at the Hotel Atlantisch seemed not to notice or to care. She stared at the document for a moment before returning it to him without a word, then took the room key from the hook on the wall behind her and placed the thirty guilders he gave her in the drawer behind the desk.

THREE DAYS LATER HE watched the coast of England rise in the west. He took a mouthful of sea air and felt the tapping of joy touch his heart for the first time since Munich. The documents he carried identified him as Julius DeGroote. He'd barely slept the previous night, cramped and nervous in his berth below deck, fearful that he'd be caught and identified, but now his confidence grew as the line on the horizon deepened, and the dream that had carried him this far suddenly seemed ready to be made real. Within days of arriving in London he'd find someone to tell his remarkable story to. The authorities at Westminster would be notified. He'd be sent for and interrogated, his information confirmed, and before long his heroic deed would be celebrated and used to inspire and embolden those back home.

As the *Eendracht* entered the outer reaches of the Thames estuary he saw the young German woman he'd met in one of the cafeterias only yesterday. Her name was Rosa Bauer. She was travelling with her daughter.

He'd heard the two talking about the stuffed bear seated in the girl's lap that first afternoon, an hour out from Rotterdam. The bear was not feeling well, the girl said. It was the rocking of the ship. The mother placed her wrist against the stuffed animal's forehead and belly and said the bear would get better soon, it was nothing serious. There were dark circles under the woman's eyes. When she tried to smile for the girl, Elser saw the fear in her face and wondered what she'd been forced to give in order to receive the two entry visas that had got her and her daughter on board.

He'd taken a seat across from them and introduced himself, then produced an imaginary medicine bottle from his breast pocket. He pinched it between two fingers and shook it with great drama.

"May I use this?" he asked, indicating the spoon beside the girl's plate. She nodded without speaking, her eyes wide with interest.

He twisted open the cap on the bottle and poured the invisible medicine into the spoon, then offered it to the bear. The girl's eyes lit up. There was no bottle or medicine, she insisted. She'd soon be six and was already clever enough to see that there was no medicine, she said.

He allowed a look of confusion to fall over his face.

Here was medicine enough for all four of them, he said, let alone this tiny bear.

The mother reached across the table and shook his hand and told him her name. Rosa, she said.

He poured out a spoonful and passed it to her and she took it and slurped it down. "It's not so bad," she said.

He took his own sip after that, and then the girl and the bear took their own imaginary draughts too.

Out on the deck now, he watched Rosa Bauer and her daughter tossing bread crusts to a trio of gulls following at the stern, the birds trailing the ship like a stringless kite. He watched the girl and her mother and the low-lying beaches and salt marshes to the north. The sea was choppy and silt-coloured, but the sun was up now, and the hundreds of barrage balloons, rooted to the ground by their heavy steel cables, hung over London like a flotilla of stubborn black clouds.

Weeks earlier he'd found a small dictionary under a café table on Rochussenstraat. He removed it from his jacket and looked up *Fliegen.* To fly. *Füttern.* To feed. *Ankommen.* To arrive. And then the whales made their appearance.

The girl and her mother joined a dozen or more passengers collecting at the railing to witness this good omen. He'd never seen such a thing before. It was marvellous how they seemed not to care about the ship. There were four or five of them breaching and slipping away again. He watched this for a moment, entranced, and turned the pages of the dictionary and drew his finger down, searching. He doubted it would carry a word as impractical as this. But here it was, *whale,* and not so different from the word in his own language, and he was pleased not only for the good omen but that the girl was here to see this wondrous spectacle.

The wind was gathering now, the whales still cutting the surface, when the three planes came out of the east, above the array of balloons.

What appeared to be a man emerged from the lead plane and wobbled, as if momentarily unnerved by this great altitude, and began to hurtle down at speed until a chute emerged and grabbed the air to slow its descent.

The backs of the whales slipped under the surface and were gone.

The three planes continued on above the barrage balloons for a short time before the spectacular burst of light filled the morning with the heat of a desert sun.

The low rumbling rocked the ship. He felt it in his bones. A billowing cloud pushed against the heavens in ripening layers of green and red and blue and rose higher and turned grey and white as its form boiled, then collapsed into itself in an odd mushroom shape.

The violent winds raised schools of herring and scad and mackerel from the churning waters, and the deck of the *Eendracht* shifted, and the air jumped alive with things that had never flown before.

1960

I discovered early in my school days that volunteering to wipe down a chalkboard or to restack books in the library did a lot to save me from the humiliations of recess. By eighth grade I'd learned to keep my head down. I hid in coatrooms, shadowed hallways, under the stairs that led to the boiler room. I cowered in the science lab storeroom with the gutted frogs and nervous mice as they awaited our cruel experiments. I hid in all these places and more, but the hall monitors and librarians and janitors were on to me. They saw through my camouflage, strategies, and excuses, and when one of them found me, or if a boy caught me loitering in the washroom, there was nothing left but to take my fate into my own hands and step out into the chaos of the schoolyard. I often gravitated to the south end of the playground where the few other German kids at school, similarly flushed from their hiding places, bided their time in retreat to await the merciful clanging of the bell.

The day the inspectors came to town that year I'd found a quiet place in the schoolyard to read my newest edition of *Revenge of Doctor Atom,* a favourite comic book in those days, and fell headlong into the story.

It told of the adventures of a man who'd been altered by the radiation that had killed so many in London. He'd not only survived the catastrophe, its effects had given him superhuman powers. With nothing more than a focused stare he was able to burn a man into a heap of ash where he stood. He was an avenger in the night, slashing through the London fog like an English Zorro. He brought chaos to the occupiers, killing officers with his laser-eyes, thwarting the Nazi menace at every turn. For me, Doctor Atom was the greatest superhero in the Atlas Comics lineup. There were many others, of course, but none could touch the righteous fury of the hero whose young wife and baby had been vaporized in the blast.

The spell of the story I'd fallen into was broken that day when a shadow darkened my open page. I turned and saw the German boy named Toby standing behind me.

"It's all just a big fat lie anyway," he said.

He had short, pudgy fingers and a crescent-shaped mustard stain on his chin.

"It's not supposed to be real. It's a comic book," I said.

"I'm not talking about that. The bomb, I mean. It's a hoax. Like that place you go to. It's just full of retarded people."

There were many things you might do or say in the schoolyard that could get you in deep trouble. What Toby had just told me was near the top of the list. I told him he'd better shut his mouth. We'd both get a licking if someone heard him talking like that. But he was undeterred. There was no such thing as that sort of bomb, he said. Not ever. He knew this because his father and uncle had told him so. They said it was nothing but a lie that gave people a reason to hate us even more than they already did. I didn't like it when he said "us." I didn't like being grouped in with him and his ilk, but of course as Germans we were all the same. I'd heard this argument before—that the bomb, and the bombing itself, was nothing but anti-German propaganda. We'd been warned against it, cautioned never to repeat the ugly lies that the German apologists attempted to spread among us. I stole a quick look to see who was watching. Boys from our class were throwing a tennis ball against the side of the building and calling out their threats and dares. To the right of this a small clowder of girls, coats off and ponytails bouncing, played Cat and Mouse in a bright blur of swirling pink jump rope.

We knew not to associate with other German kids at school. It was always best to keep to yourself. By the time I'd reached fifth grade it was more than clear to me that Thomas had been right about us never making any friends at all. I don't remember feeling especially sorry for myself about this. It was how it had to be back then. To ease our way through those days Thomas and I had our secret communication. We sent each other signals when we could, even if we weren't able to meet directly. There were notes we dropped for each other, and hand gestures we shared, and sometimes just seeing him there across the schoolyard, handling a boy the way he knew how—he was always good with his fists—shored up my sagging spirits. He'd often come to my rescue in the early days, but by the time I was in seventh grade he was too busy fighting his own battles, and I was not so young that I shouldn't be able to take care of myself.

"It's called propaganda. Official lies. You know. BS!" Toby said.

The girls were still skipping but the boys with the tennis ball had splintered off into smaller groups. The yard monitor was standing at the centre of a second group of kids, her hair tied in a tight bun, blowing cigarette smoke over their obedient heads. I shrank behind my copy of *Doctor Atom*.

"*Es ist nur britische Propaganda,*" Toby said.

Glancing over my shoulder, I begged him to be quiet. There were only two things worse than lying about those people under care down on Radiation Row, and speaking German in the schoolyard was one of them. The truth as I knew it was as real as Toby's pudgy fingers. I knew it for all sorts of reasons. I knew it because I'd seen pictures and films about London and the European Clearances and the sprawling Madagascar ghettos. I knew it because everyone hated the Germans, and the Germans deserved every bit of that hatred. Göring was a blimp of a man by then. Our teacher made much of that. "Here we have an example of the *supe-*

rior German race," she would say, holding up the latest newspaper cartoon that showed him, in one case, gorging himself at a banquet table cut in the shape of Europe. The classroom erupted in laughter, and the girl seated in the desk next to mine puffed out her cheeks at me.

I'd heard my mother's stories about Mercy House and seen those blind souls at Chisolm Square with my own eyes. It was a fact so real and so urgent that my heart threatened to jump out of my chest when he said that lie; worse yet, he'd spoken the lie in German.

The official ban on the German language had been lifted by then, but the stigma lived on. In the street it earned you a nasty look or a bloody nose, and in the schoolyard there was always a boy eager to take you on if he heard you speak it, which no one had ever been stupid enough to do—until that morning.

The name of the yard monitor that day was Miss Fields. I found her by the sandpit, next to the three small cedars that looked to me like prehistoric creatures, their roots and limbs twisting and animal-like.

"And what did he say?" she asked. "What did he say in that filthy tongue of yours?" She grabbed my arm and asked a second time, and the girls who always accompanied her as she patrolled the yard began to chant, "Tell us your mind, or your eyes will turn blind!"

I was wearing the brown corduroy coat my mother had used half our clothing-ration book to purchase for me only a week earlier. I was very proud of it—it looked almost new. When her fingernails dug through the material into my arm I wasn't as aware of the flash of pain that raced through me as I was fearful that she might tear my new second-hand coat, and that I'd have to explain this to my mother.

Miss Fields marched me over to where poor Toby Schwabe waited after I told her what I'd heard. He'd been watching the whole time, of course, his face pale with fear. He stood still as a tree awaiting his fate. There was nowhere to run. A dozen boys in any corner of the schoolyard would have gladly caught him and pushed his face in the mud.

He began to cry when she told him to repeat what he'd said. More kids were gathering around now, and they began to chant the rhyme they'd called at me—*Tell us your mind, or your eyes will turn blind.* When he finally did, she pinched and twisted his ear and hauled him off to the principal's office, his footsteps clipped and infant-like beside her brutal athletic stride.

I was not proud of myself, of course. But I'd done what I needed to do to spare myself the licking he'd get. I saw him again an hour later seated on the bench outside the office. His ear and the palms of his hands were beet-red. He wore his family's German serial number on a sign strung around his neck. I kept walking, ashamed of my treachery.

A group of boys was waiting for me as I rounded a corner. One of them pushed me up against a locker.

"Kraut bastard," he said.

This boy's name was Larson. He was two grades ahead of me, in Thomas's year, and a full head taller.

"Nothing to say for yourself?"

He gave me another good shove and raised me off my feet and slammed me up higher against the locker door.

"What're you going to do, Teufel? Where's your big brother now?" He dropped me to my feet and stepped back and raised his fists. The other boys pressed in.

These were the sons of those who roamed the town on Remembrance Day night setting fires and breaking bottles. My father had cautioned against any confrontation with these boys. I was supposed to back away even when they taunted and hazed me and threatened to knock me down.

Larson leaned into my face and growled. "So say it, say it now. Tell me what your name means." He cocked his head and held his fist under my chin. "You've got three seconds."

I told him with a second to spare.

"That's right. William Devil. And don't you forget it," he said.

He relaxed his fist and raised his arm to salute me. The other boys followed his example. It seemed like everyone in the hallway then gave me a mocking *Sieg Heil* salute—the one we'd seen a thousand times in the films we were obliged to watch. I'd only ever felt shame at the sight of people doing this. But I felt something else now. It was anger and frustration and fear. My father's cautions and any good sense in my head abandoned me. I swung and caught Larson in the eye with a fist—it was a lucky shot, I suppose, eliciting a lovely popping sound—and he dropped to a knee and brought his hands to his face.

Exhilarated, I waited for him to get up, or for the next boy to come at me. The crowd parted, as if by magic, and Miss Fields grabbed me by that same arm and dug in her nails. I was not wearing my coat this time. The yelp of pain that escaped my throat caused the boys who watched this to laugh.

"Your efforts today to ignite a third world war have proven successful, Herr Teufel. But your kind will not win this one, you can be sure of it," she said. She dug her nails even deeper into my flesh and marched me down the hall, past Toby, who was still sitting on the bench nursing his hands and rubbing his ear, and roughly guided me into the principal's office.

It was a small, cramped space that barely accommodated his cluttered desk. On the east wall was the window from which the principal liked to watch us kids during recess. Next to the window was a portrait of Tommy Douglas, the prairie boy prime minister, as my father liked to call him, who by now, well into his third term, had welcomed Khrushchev to Ottawa more than half a dozen times. My father liked nothing at all about the Communists, and the buffoonish Khrushchev even less, other than the fact that they seemed to hate the Nazis as much as we did. They were the bulwark against the forces that might eat us alive, and even the incident in our

House of Commons that previous summer, when the Soviet First Secretary had removed his shoe and banged it repeatedly on the table, was easily tolerated in exchange for the ongoing aid and assistance that guaranteed our survival.

I wasn't thinking about politics as I stood there, though, waiting for the punishment that was coming my way. I feared the principal more than I feared anyone else at school, far more than I feared even the toughest boys in our hallways. Formally of the Highland Light Infantry, he had no sympathy for me and my brother, or for any of the other German kids under his charge, few as we were. He'd lost an eye in the war, and that empty socket, hidden beneath its black oval patch, terrified me almost as much as the eyes of those poor souls we saw in Chisolm Square on Remembrance Day. As I waited I listened to the sound of the janitor sloshing out his squeeze-mop in the hallway. He was cleaning the boy's blood and snot from the floor, I imagined. I feared I'd be expelled, and this would lead to my father having problems at work. I'd fantasized countless times about not having to go to school. But now the idea of staying in my room for the rest of my life turned my stomach to knots. I lurched for the bin in the corner and threw up just as Principal Crouse and Miss Fields came through the door, the boy I'd knocked down huddled between them.

Miss Fields told Larson to take the bin outside to the janitor and come back immediately. When he returned, Crouse made some effort to examine the boy's face, then stepped behind his desk and produced a cowhide strap from the top drawer. It was half the length of a belt and twice as thick—so thick and tough that it stayed straight when he held it at one end.

He slapped it gently into his palm as he approached me, and tested it against the surface of his desk with a stinging snap. He offered it to Larson, telling him to give it a go, but Larson just stared down at his feet. The principal waited, shook his head in disgust, and brought the leather strap down against his desk a second time. He told me to present my hands, palms up, and proceeded to administer my punishment.

He held my wrist with one hand while he struck with the other. When he was through with it, seven lashings per hand, he gave me a paper towel to wipe away the blood and told me to wait on the bench outside the office. I made sure I didn't cry, though I wanted to more than anything in the world. Toby was still there, condemned for his own trespass, staring at the opposite wall with a scared look on his face. We didn't look at each other, though I saw him sneaking peeks at my hands as I tried to wrap them with the paper towel I'd been given.

I was wearing my own sign now. It was a cardboard placard secured around my neck that read 169061-4, the number painted on the front door of our house. I sat there for an hour or so, afraid to move a muscle. Thomas walked past twice, but always someone was watching, and on the third pass, when the hallway was clear, he was able to hand off the note he'd written for me. *Inspection day today. NOW!* it said.

Skipping class was one thing; leaving the bench before you were released was another. I felt like I was dying. I dared not imagine the punishment the principal would meet me with the following day if I left the bench before he released me. Added to that, a hallway full of kids had seen me throw that punch, and the boy I'd knocked down wasn't the toughest at school by any stretch. Others would come for me. And I had defied my father's injunction to never throw the first punch. In all the Remembrance Days past, he'd never once confronted those men who gathered on our lawn. It would only make things worse, he said. It would prove their point: once a German, always a German. I wouldn't be able to hide the strap marks on my hands for long, and once he saw what I'd done he'd remind me that this act of defiance would now be on my permanent school record. I would be considered an instigator. More than this, word of my defiance would likely follow him back to the shipyard—where one day, if I was lucky enough, I might be placed in an apprenticeship program.

I watched the clock on the wall opposite the bench. The portrait of the Queen stared back at me. It was as if she knew what I'd do, the mischief in my veins too strong to rein in. I couldn't help myself. It was inbred, this disagreeable German spirit, integral to who I was. I would cause problems, though I didn't want to. I looked down the hallway, then up. It was empty but for a girl who appeared at that moment. Her name was Mary-Beth. She was one of those arid, doleful girls who travelled the schoolyard at recess in Miss Fields's wake, throwing superior glances as they went. She took more pleasure than most in ridiculing me. When she saw me, she stuck out her tongue and spun off around the corner. The decision was made for me, it seemed. I'd never win, no matter what.

I found Thomas waiting at the bike racks five minutes later. He held my hands in his, looked closely, and shook his head.

"Jesus, Dad's going to kill you," he said.

There was no need to remind me. I wasn't looking forward to the end of the day. I'd make my confession, and my father would sit me down for a lecture about the precarious situation we were all in, every day of our lives. It was up to us to show our neighbours that we were not the people they thought we were. You know better, he'd say, and then he'd leave me to think about what I'd done. But all I cared about right now was getting down to Mercy House and seeing what those inspectors had in store for us that afternoon.

There were not as many kids waiting that day as there usually were. Eight or nine boys lingered at the side of the road smoking their stolen cigarettes and horking at the low-hanging branches of a dead cherry tree as they watched the trucks parked on the circular drive and the men who waved their Geiger counters over the property, tracing window frames and downspouts and the front and side entrances. We heard the telltale crackle from the device held by the man who tested the small fountain at the centre of the drive. He removed something from a pocket and dipped it in the water and placed it again in his pocket. As they often did, two sisters and a man in a dark suit stood on the doorstep watching this until the team was ready to enter, and the door closed behind them, and there they stayed unseen by us for longer than usual.

Thomas and I stood off from the other boys, as we always did. They kept to themselves in groups of two or three, spitting and mumbling nervously as they waited for something to happen. My hands were still burning from the strapping. Another cigarette was lit and passed around. The smoke smelled good, and though I hated these boys I admired the imperfect smoke rings they were somehow able to create. I envied them their nonchalance and their cool, uncaring nature and wondered if I'd ever be as lucky as them to live in a place where you knew you belonged. And then something unusual happened as we waited. They seemed to get bored. The one who'd lit the cigarette flicked it in the air and declared the fun was over. He and another two boys left the group and started up the road. Soon the others were gone, too, and Thomas and I were alone.

We were not so easily deterred or bored. For a moment, as the last of them left, I'd felt superior to these boys whose determination had so suddenly and surprisingly failed them. We were the only ones now, the connection we felt to the house still strong. We waited another half hour until the first of the inspectors re-emerged, and then the others appeared. They carried the black bags we always saw them with to the backs of the trucks. The sisters and the man in the suit returned to their positions at the entrance, as if seeing off departing visitors, and after the inspectors had packed away their gear they climbed into the two vehicles and the roar of motors sounded and the trucks began up the lane towards us.

The Russian trucks had a wide, imposing front bumper and grille and tires as thick as tree trunks. This was the same make we'd always see in the short propaganda films in school that trumpeted the evolution of Canadian-Soviet cooperation. Their diesel engines grew louder as they approached. The earth rumbled with their weight and the cool April air vibrated with sound. There were two men up front, driver and passenger, and in the back of each under the tarp there were three or four more.

The man in the passenger seat of the first truck was not smiling. I didn't recognize him from any of the previous years. Perhaps he was new or usually sat in the back with the samples and equipment they used. He was a young man with sharp features and light blue eyes, with a crewcut and black horn-rimmed glasses. He held a cigarette between his fingers, right arm hanging out the open window. He nodded and slapped his hand twice against the door when he saw me and my brother standing at the side of the road.

The truck slowed and stopped, and he threw open his door and climbed down and walked over to us. He looked at me as if I were another sample he might consider for transport back to the laboratory.

Something about the moment brought a smile to his face—I didn't know what yet—and I decided that he was a nice man. He was probably still in his twenties, younger than my father, certainly, and had straight white teeth and a dimple in his chin, like my grandfather, whose picture sat in the glass cabinet in the living room. He smelled of cigarette smoke and strong soap and rubber—I imagined from the gloves he'd been wearing until a few minutes ago.

"Doctor Atom," he said in heavily accented English. Then he turned to the man in the truck and said something in rapid-fire Russian. The man behind the wheel nodded.

"You like Doctor Atom?" he said, turning back to me and pointing with his cigarette to the comic book in my hand. I'd been flipping through it as we waited for the men to emerge from the house; it was rolled in a tube in my hand but loose enough to show the flash of Doctor Atom's eyes in the cover illustration.

The Russian inspector noticed my palms now, still torn and bloody from my strapping, and said something I did not understand. His language was coarse and hard in my ear. He waited a moment, then took hold of my left wrist and examined the cuts there. I tried to show that I wasn't afraid, of him or the pain, but he must have seen it there in my face. He shook his head, with pity or confusion or concern, I have no idea, then took a pull on his cigarette and drew the smoke deep into his lungs and held it there long enough that I began to wonder if time had stood still. But now he did something surprising. He breathed his cigarette smoke over the cut on my palm in a long grey breath. He squeezed my wrist while the smoke poured over my cuts, and when there was no smoke left he let go and smiled at me, as if I were in on the joke. His colleague in the idling truck honked the horn and called out to him and he released me, his lungs emptied, and tousled my hair like a coach congratulating a kid who'd hit a decent drive out into midfield.

"Doctor Atom—it's you now," he said.

My hand didn't look or feel different, of course, but everything was different now. It was still red and hurt like hell but he'd blown his radiation breath into my wounds, and now the worst was to come. *Now it's you.* My superstitious heart slammed against my chest. I couldn't help myself. I'd spent a lifetime in the shadow of that house on Radiation Row, heard the hundreds of tales, seen the newsreels, and watched those blind-staring eyes as its helpless occupants caned their way through Chisolm Square on Remembrance Day. I made a fist, then shook out my hand, trying to undo what he'd just done to me.

He walked back to the truck, climbed in, and slammed the door shut. The engine roared and the truck started to move. He flicked his cigarette out the cab window. It landed in the grass beside the road. I waited till they were up the road a stretch, then dropped my comic book and ran down to the lake and washed my hand as best I could. It helped the stinging but it wasn't enough, the radiation was already inside me.

I walked back up the steep short incline to the road where I found Thomas waiting for me. I don't recall what he was doing when all this happened. He would have been right there, as he always was, but my attention had been fixed on the Russian's face. I didn't tell my brother what I was thinking. I was too frightened. I got on my bike and said I was going home, I needed to get home right away, and that's when I looked up and saw someone watching us from a second-floor window of the old house.

It was far off, as I say, but even at that distance I could see that the figure wasn't wearing the habit—the white bib and coif and black veil and dress—always worn by the nursing sisters, in spring, summer, fall, and winter, as though the suffering they were exposed to rendered their own discomfort trivial by comparison, which without doubt it surely was. I could make out no details beyond that, not even enough to know if this was a man or a woman. The figure held still after I got Thomas's attention. He turned and we both stared, and then the person waved to us.

Cowards both, we dropped our bikes and crouched behind the fieldstone wall. It was an impulse, foolish of course, yet I was overcome with a strange feeling that I later understood was humiliation. The shock of our discovery—that we'd been found out—and the impossible realization that we'd been spotted by a *blind* person began to take root. In a moment all we knew about the house made no sense at all. We held still, our backs hugging the stone, not daring to lift our heads up to peek again. Thomas stared at me with drowning eyes. He arched his shoulders in a questioning gesture, as if to say he had no idea at all what we'd just seen. We'd been caught at our own game, it seemed, no longer the observers but the observed, and by whom and for what reason we had no clue.

I SCRUBBED MY HAND in blistering hot water when I got home. The superstitions that ruled us, ridiculous to think of now, were as real to me as the smells of our mother's cooking that filled the house that late afternoon. The wounds were opened again with the scrubbing, the washbasin pink with blood. It was an irrefutable fact. I might even have felt some dizziness come over me, so convinced was I that the radiation that had felled half the city of London was now churning the blood in my veins.

My mother was standing at the kitchen sink. "What's that face?" she said in German, and she asked if something was wrong. She couldn't see my hands, stuffed painfully as they were in my pockets. I slouched, shaking my head. She asked if I wanted to take over pressing the potatoes. She was making dumplings, a dish that my father and I loved more than any other. I'd be back in a minute, I told her. There was a light switch at the top of the stairs, but I didn't turn it on when I went down to the basement; I waited in the dark and stared at my hand, thinking that the radiation I'd absorbed might make it glow.

I was sitting on the plywood shipping crate my father had built years ago for the things we'd take with us if Germany ever became a normal country again and my mother was allowed to go home. It was a symbol of hope that he offered her, that he was with her in this dream of hers, though I'm sure both of them understood plainly enough that this could never happen. Now that shipping crate held the winter coats and skates and scarves and mittens that smelled of mothballs when we retrieved them in November.

The crate was set against the west wall, in a corner of the basement yellowed by the ribbon of light coming down from the top of the stairs. The horsehair plaster wall behind it was crumbling, and overhead the exposed timbers in the low ceiling ran crossways, strung with ancient black wires that fed electricity to the floors above. There was nothing down there for me but solitude and the dark I'd trusted would reveal the radiation poisoning that now coursed through my veins. I stayed put for as long as possible, holding one split hand in the other, until my mother's shadow appeared at the top of the stairs and I heard her calling down to me.

She found out about the hands, of course. You can hide

that sort of thing from your mother for only so long. She saw me favouring one and took my wrist and pried open my fingers and asked who'd done this to me. Eventually, when I told her, she said this was a country run by animals and she would be marching me up to the school—she said all this in a rush of German. I begged her not to go to the school, it would only make things worse for me.

She took me to the kitchen sink, where she cleaned me up as best she could, and then she turned away and began to cry softly.

I knew she was crying for herself as much as she was for me. I told her it wasn't as bad as it looked and took the cloth from her and finished cleaning my hands, and she sat down at the kitchen table and stared out the window.

My father's good mood when he got home turned in an instant when he saw the state I was in and heard the story about the fight and the strapping, but he didn't say anything about taking me up to the school to demand an explanation or apology. Instead he said we were going to the clinic to get my hands looked after. All that other business we'd talk about later. I told him the cuts weren't so deep but he knew enough not to believe me.

I wasn't used to getting the sort of attention I got that evening from my father. The way he draped his arm over my shoulder as he led me to the car made me feel loved and cared for, and despite the fact that my hands were still burning I almost believed a strapping like that had been worth it. He was not a man given to doting or obvious displays of emotion—I imagine few fathers were in those days—but here, as he turned over the engine of the old Chevy, it seemed like this mission to get me looked after was the purest expression of love and caring I'd ever known. The feeling didn't last long.

The camp we called Little Berlin came into view ten minutes later. It was a short drive but long enough for the burning in my hands to come back after my mother had run cold water over them. I'd seen the camp up close like this only a few times, and each time it had been enough to know I didn't want to see it again. Through the barbed-wire fencing I saw the long rows of clapboard shacks, and men and women marking time. Each house was the size of a big garage and held up to three families. There were no roads or schools or shops where you could buy things, no libraries, no nothing. There were thousands of people rounded up in there waiting for who knew what. If you were lucky—this according to my father—a truck rolled in and you'd be one of a dozen or so men hired for a day job. But in no time you were back there again, staring out from behind that barbed wire, as they were doing now on that evening we drove past.

When I turned away my father slowed the car. "Take a good long look," he said. "They're just like us, no better, no worse," and when he said I should remember what it felt like to see the look of suffering on an innocent person's face, I wondered how he could be sure they were innocent. Every schoolboy in the country had been obliged to memorize the speech King George had delivered from the steps of Province House in Halifax, Nova Scotia, in September 1944, on the day the British government-in-exile declared itself alive and well, just a month after the bomb. The following day the speech was published in every newspaper across the country and throughout the Commonwealth. Since then, its most famous line had been reprinted and illustrated and hung in public halls and factories in every city and town across the land. *A viper is nonetheless a viper no matter where the egg is hatched.* The posters that hung in our school cafeteria bearing this line in red lettering showed a bloody hand strangling a serpent. Decades of immigration to the Commonwealth had failed to loosen the bond that the Germans here felt for their country of origin, the King had said that day in Halifax. A German was a German, no matter how long they lived among us, no matter how many generations removed from the Fatherland they were. There would be no such thing as a free German in all of the Commonwealth, he'd said, not while the people of the British Isles suffered under the boot of fascism.

We didn't speak of these things in our home or dwell on the idea of German treachery as the King would have us do. I did my best to ignore the poster that hung in the school cafeteria and the many others we saw around town, as I'd tried to turn my eyes away from those Germans who watched us from inside the camp that evening.

The clinic was a sorry-looking building of weather-stained

stucco we'd had occasion to visit two or three times, once when Thomas broke an arm falling off his bike. It was the last place I wanted to go now—a black hole that served only to remind me of the hard conditions we lived under. It served the population of Little Berlin, which at the time numbered in the thousands, but it was not inside the gates of the camp itself. I stood silently while my father argued for the attention of a physician. Finally we were led to an examination room where a Russian doctor looked at my hands, covered them with a cream of some sort, and wrapped them in an iodoform gauze. He didn't care to ask what had happened. He was not there because he wanted to be, tending to sick and dying Germans. The contempt the Russians held us in was as deep as anyone's here. I wanted to tell him that one of his countrymen had breathed smoke into the wound after emerging from Mercy House so he could tell me that there was no need to worry, that this was just a lot of superstition running around in my head. But I wasn't able to say a thing. I slipped down off the examination table, and my father led me back out to the parking lot.

It was close to dark when we got home. I managed not to cry until I was alone in my bedroom, and then Thomas came looking for me and said I didn't deserve what had happened to me, none of us did. I went downstairs again when everyone was asleep and looked for a bottle of bee pollen in the kitchen cupboards. I didn't know what such a bottle would look like, but knew its contents had protected my mother against the radiation at Mercy House. She'd talked about putting charcoal powder in her tea, too. I didn't know where else to look for either of these things, or if I'd even know them to see them. Taking care to favour my gauzed hands, I climbed on the kitchen counter and searched our cupboards. I found nothing of interest but for a loaded mousetrap, which made me jump with fright when it snapped back there in the dark.

1944

The *Eendracht* sat at anchor for three days in a windless calm. On the fourth morning the northerlies brought the first smells of rot and decay. He smelled it on deck as he watched the flattened city. He smelled it in his cabin and on his clothes and in the food he ate in the stunned silence of the cafeteria. Soon it was everywhere, a taste he could not spit out. The landscape smouldered on after the fires were down, the cloud hanging over it like the very Hand of God. Slowly it began to break apart, drifting eastward to Southend-on-Sea and finally out over the Channel.

At night the city was black as coal, vanished from the face of the earth, yet along the length of the river the constellations of campfires grew.

On the fifth morning he watched a young man heave himself over the ship's railing—an attempt to swim to shore, or to die, he could not know which. At length the figure disappeared from view, arms pinwheeling against the current. The whales did not appear again but the gulls arrived now, fattened on the dead, and took their rest on the ledges of the upper decks where they preened their dirty feathers.

The smouldering was gone now but the smoke and charred smell presided over the estuary. On board, the breakdown was already well underway. Elser noticed it midway through the fourth afternoon. Groups of men collected. In the cafeterias and common rooms, impromptu assemblies gathered, alliances forming to plot a course of action. The captain attempted to maintain order, but chaos spread through the ship. Some wanted to steam for South America, others to return to Rotterdam to take their chances there. The sergeant-at-arms made three arrests that day. On the fifth day he himself was placed in the brig after six members of the crew took control of the ship. The engines were turned over for the first time in days and the *Eendracht* began to move.

Elser felt the vibrations of the steel plates underfoot and saw the shoreline slowly slip away. He wondered if the men who'd taken control had opted for a return to Holland. In the evening, the fires that dotted the estuary shoreline grew distant and pale, but it was impossible to gather from this position what direction the ship was headed.

Around midnight he heard shots fired somewhere below the wheelhouse. The engines fell silent again and remained so for the rest of the night.

He broke apart items of furniture in his cabin and selected a pointed fragment of chair-leg and held it in his hand as he lay listening for footsteps in the passageway on the other side of his door. In the morning he came up on deck and saw a German frigate a thousand yards off their portside.

THE UNCONDITIONAL SURRENDER WAS announced that afternoon over the wireless. Even without any knowledge of English, Elser heard defeat in the prime minister's voice. The war was lost, and all British forces would begin demobilization at once.

"The history of mankind has never seen a weapon of such destructive power as the one used against us," Churchill said, "and no race so determined to rain down fury upon the heads of its enemy. Let there be no shame, only great sorrow. Defeat is one miserable truth. Disgrace is another. These times have laid us low. But they have not robbed us of the moral courage that binds us. Great Britain is evermore the land of honour and freedom, and one day we shall see new light. Now we will remember our greatest triumphs in our nation's gravest hour. Never will history record that in these days a people so noble deserted her principles. And that is our victory. Today, in the midst of suffering and danger, our resolve is steadfast, our sorrows great."

A boarding party arrived from the frigate and took command of the *Eendracht* the following morning. It was an orderly process. Elser waited on the aft deck among the passengers and crew while the German officer who led the party carried out his inspections, nodding with the look on his face of a hunter taking in the full appreciation of his day's work.

WITHIN HOURS THE SHIP put in at the eastern basin of St. Katharine Docks alongside a wrecked paddle steamer turned on its side, the rusted hull blown open like tissue paper. Elser was with the first of the work gangs that were taken ashore and marched a hundred yards into the burned city, where they were put to work clearing a roadway of bodies and burned-out car wrecks and heaps of brick and stone and twisted metal. They worked until full dark, and that night Elser sheltered with twenty other men on the second floor of a building whose east wall lay in a heaping pile in the street. He sat in a room that looked out over the emptiness, speechless and exhausted, and wept at the devastation brought down on this city.

THE FOLLOWING DAY, A blizzard of leaflets fell from the sky and settled like snow all around him:

THE WAR IS OVER
CHURCHILL IS IN CUSTODY
THE ENGLISH ARE DEFEATED

They worked on through that day, the wind scuttling the leaflets along the street, and at twilight their guards marched them underground to a tube station already crowded with survivors of the bomb. The long, narrow space was grey-lit with torches that illuminated the ghost-like figures spread out before him. He found a narrow path and sat and watched as a lone man appeared from the darkness at one end of the tunnel pulling a two-wheeled shopping cart in which sat, as if in a cage, a child of perhaps four or five. The man wore Wellingtons and a black tuxedo suit jacket and what looked to be pyjama bottoms, torn and smeared with soot. The child in the cart stared at the people on the platform as the man wheeled her past along the rutted track. Seated on the platform, Elser watched him walk the rails over the length of the station, the cart lurching against each tie, from one end to the other, until the man and his burden faded again into darkness.

IN THE MORNING THE German soldiers marched them back up into the grey light of day, where they were fed watery soup and skillet bread at a two-wheeled field kitchen pulled by a half-starved quarter horse. Elser ate quickly and watched the thin stems of smoke rising all around them and believed hell would look no different. He stored in his pocket the crusts that remained when the order was given to fall in. They were marched through the ruins and put to work clearing the stretch of road that reached north from

London Bridge to Monument Square and the great Doric column that still stood there, everything else between the river and the column razed to the ground. Their guards stood upwind from where they worked collecting bodies while they cleared the roadway of wrecked cars and rubble. Nearing midday Elser saw a woman and man cradling a child, huddled together at the base of the column, their faces blank with terror. The child was sleeping or dead, he could not tell, but after these eight days the burns on its body seemed to continually boil, as if the bomb's fire was still alight in its victim's flesh.

He removed the crusts of bread from his pocket and placed them on the ground for the man and woman and backed away.

It was from that point on that he began to wonder if there was some connection between this strange new fire and the frequent rotation he'd begun to notice in the soldiers who drove them on through these ruins. Their guards served only half a day before they were replaced by a new squad of soldiers. He'd not spoken a word for fear he'd be discovered, but he listened for anything that might help him understand what was happening in the world beyond these smoking heaps of rubble, and if this bomb he'd watched fall from the sky had been loaded with some new incendiary that lingered on past its first impact. He heard the soldiers talk of their relief that the war was over, and that they were eager to get home now as much as anyone, but he did not hear them speak about the bomb or the survivors, whose wounds were like nothing he'd seen before.

IN THE DAYS THAT followed he saw the shadows burned into the pavements, and later he learned that these had once been people, and that the odd geometry burned into the skin of some of the survivors reflected the patterns of the clothing they'd been wearing on that morning the bomb fell from the sky. He learned to quickly rifle through the pockets of the dead when the guards weren't watching, though he knew three men in his work gang had already been shot for looting, the world now operating at these strange extremes where the chance of pulling a biscuit or a penknife from a dead man's pocket was worth the risk. Usually he ate any food he found right away, but the roll of Parma Violets he discovered in a young woman's handbag kept him going for days. At night, among the weeping on the platform of the tube station, and later when they migrated north, deeper into the city, he'd sneak one from the cellophane wrap he'd secreted in his waistband and hold it under his tongue for as long as it lasted. He'd imagine another place in another time, eyes closed and far away, and he'd keep them closed for as long as he could before the taste of ash crept back over his tongue.

One night as he held the candy under his tongue he heard his guards speaking of the penal colony called Madagascar that would begin receiving Jews from across Europe before the new year. In an instant the illusion he'd harboured slipped away and he imagined the horrors that might be unleashed back home, now that this madness could find its final expression.

SOMETIMES THE THINGS HE took away with him weren't edible or practical at all but simply offered some temporary distraction from the world around him. With the pocket watch he found under a collapsed wall north of the Doric column he imagined the Illinois Watch Company as it might have been back at the turn of the century, the early 1890s if he read its markings right, and the places it had travelled to until it finally arrived and died here in this city, its two intact hands stopped forever at eight-fifteen.

The living were worse off than the dead by now, weeks after the bomb. He still found them sometimes, up there in those piles of brick, and carried them down to the street and laid them out for help to come. But the doctors arriving from all over England worked day and night in the aid stations that began to appear throughout the city, and so those people he tried to help received no help at all until the wagons came to collect the dead.

WHEN HE OVERHEARD A young soldier, speaking in Low Saxon, refer to something called "radiation" twenty days into his recruitment, he wondered if this was the thing that fuelled the fires that seemed to boil on under the skin or erupt into scabs and scarring of frightening proportions. The two men listening to the soldier warmed their coffee over a cook-fire as he spoke. It was neither a pestilence nor a poison gas but an after-effect of the weapon they were celebrating back home, he said, a danger so persistent that each German squad could serve only six hours at a time.

AT FIRST ELSER DIDN'T notice the slow creep of blindness that began to consume him a month or so into his ordeal, and when he did he was able to convince himself that the blurring in his left eye was a result of his starvation diet and the deep exhaustion that consumed him. He'd seen the opaqueness gathering over the eyes of some of the men he worked alongside and told himself this would not be his fate. He would not end up as one of those poor devils sitting helplessly in a ditch, the pearl-like blankness drawn over their eyes like curtains, but in the days leading into November the vision in his right eye began to dim too, and from that time on the world around him began to fall into darkness.

THE GERMAN TRANSPORTS ANCHORED off Sunset Park and West New Brighton continued to disgorge their divisions and equipment as the Channel fell to its autumn storms. The advance commando units that spread through the city in the early days after the signing of the unconditional surrender on board the *Scharnhorst* worked in short, brutal rotations cleaning up the last of the resistance that remained before shipping off again to one of the troop carriers at anchor in the Thames estuary, where they scrubbed down and swallowed the iodine pills they were told were another variation on the Pervitin they'd been taking since their push through Europe began. They worked in conjunction with the British Union of Fascists and the English Bund Society, who in the early years of the war had met in basements and alleyways but would now ascend to the very heights of political power in this new England.

On the steps of Parliament House in Edinburgh, William Gilmour of the Scottish Democratic Fascist Party declared the triumph of Scottish independence and the death of the English liberal class. There was talk now of the end of the Bolshevik menace, and finally the Jewish problem could be seen to with a firm hand. Those who'd lain in wait seized their opportunity. Sir Oswald Mosley, disgraced Member of Parliament for Smethwick and leader of the British Union of Fascists, was released from house arrest and summoned to Berlin. He was received by Chancellor Göring, who later that day spoke on the wireless to the people of Great Britain of the wave of National Socialism that was now crashing over the British Isles and of the heroic new generation of leaders that would carry their proud nation into the future.

ELSER ROSE TO HIS feet when the kapos came along the platform kicking and swinging their truncheons. He blinked and shook his head, not sure he was in his own body, or that it wasn't still the middle of the night and this some drill meant to torment them further, rousing them in the pitch-darkness, so absorbing that it was absolute. Not even the miners' lights the kapos wore or the torches they carried pierced it. He hit the side of his head with his open palm, as if to activate some stalled mechanism buried there, and then, waving his hand over his eyes, he knew he was blind.

The kapos swung their truncheons and shouted their orders again and the crowd started to move along the platform. Elser raised his hands and felt along the wall and made it up the stairs into the cold morning before he fell hard against a low pile of brick and sat waiting for the guards to notice. He knew what was coming. He'd seen dozens of men like he was now—those who'd stared into the centre of the fire that day in August—shot and left for the wagons to come and collect them.

He heard the guard approach and stand over him a moment, the leather of his boots and the strap being drawn through the holster's buckle, and then he felt the Luger's muzzle against his temple.

It was God's mercy and quickly now, please. He was ready, here in this place he'd created with the killing of one monster that gave rise to another. He was responsible for all of this,

his plan turned so viciously upside down, and he felt the hands of death begin to close upon him.

He sat there at the centre of his life, waiting.

The man who should have shot him holstered his sidearm and called out that there was another one here, useless and blind as a stone.

Elser heard his footsteps moving off, and in a moment other men came and he was dragged over the broken cobble and hefted into the back of a truck.

IT WAS HOURS LATER and raining when the vehicle stopped and the German soldiers began unloading the blind. Leading them one by one to a rope tied to a post, they took each prisoner's right hand and placed it on the rope, and the left hand on the shoulder of the prisoner in front of them. The rain when Elser was brought down from the truck-bed tasted of ash and smoke and froze him to the bone, and he was added to the procession of the blind. And so the line grew until the command was given, and as one they began to move.

After seventy-eight counted steps he stumbled on stairs that led up and out of the rain into a structure that echoed with their shuffling misery. He dropped his hand from the shoulder in front of him, the chain broken, and reached into the emptiness beside him, and there on his left he felt something smooth and hard and textured with age. His fingers travelled over it and fell away to nothing as he stepped forward. He felt the same shape replicated again and then again, and he knew that he was in a church and these were the seatbacks of pews.

In his mind's eye he saw the space they moved through— the aisle, the chancel ahead, and the figure of a tortured Christ hovering somewhere above—until an English voice called out and the procession stopped and slid away by ones and twos onto the cold of the waiting benches.

The saints had been taken down from their pedestals now and the first ten rows of pews unbolted from the stone floor to make room for what became the casualty clearing station at the St. John-at-Hampstead Parish Church of the Blind. He learned its name later, and that those who tended to them in this place were a Red Cross team from Cardiff, but on the day of his arrival he knew only what he touched and smelled. There were no German voices here, once they were unloaded from the truck, that might help him understand how long he would be kept. In the early hours of his arrival and in the days that followed he tapped his throat when a voice spoke to him, as if to indicate he was mute, and out of pity or haste a hand took his and led him forward to where he was supposed to stand or sit, for how long he never knew.

AFTER THE RAINSTORM ENDED that first night, the wide, echoing space was silent but for the muted coughing

of those around him and the metallic sound of a water dripping from overhead into a tin cup or plate and the stubborn wind whistling through an opening in a blown-out
chancel window. Gone was the smell of charred and rotting
bodies, and now the cold air smelled of earth and rain and
woodsmoke. He wrapped himself in the blanket he'd been
provided and set to praying. The cold ate into his bones.
He prayed that he might find the world returned to itself
whole and intact when morning came, that none of this was
more than a haunting dream. He prayed that sight would be
restored to him and to those sprawled out around him, and
that he might be forgiven for what he'd done to set this miserable history in motion. He prayed for those he loved and
that their memory would never be lost and prayed for the
city he'd been delivered from, and when the violent shivering
seized his whole body he prayed for a dry pair of boots and
the simple warmth of a fire.

HE AWOKE HOURS LATER to the sound of a woman's
voice. At first he wondered if he was dreaming. The voice
was familiar to him, barely above a whisper. *At night when
the world is quiet our voices rise to the heavens.* His mother
had said that once. *This is why we pray at night when the
world falls still, so God can hear us better.* The voice kept on,
at prayer, he imagined. With his right hand he could have
touched the woman, she was that close, and then her name

came to him. He listened a moment longer, and then he said her name in a whisper and told her that he was the man on the ship over from Rotterdam who'd fed her and her daughter imaginary spoonfuls of medicine.

He felt her hand move. Their fingers touched.

"Is she here?" he asked. "Is she here beside you?"

When she said nothing he closed his hand over hers, both of them trembling and silent for what remained of the night.

IN THE WEEKS THAT followed they choreographed their days around the chiming of the church bell that rang as a clarion call to their misery and loss. He did not ask about the young woman's daughter after that first night. When they became separated during the day—the blind lost among the blind—the sounding bell led them back to the last arch of the north transept where they met again, and there, wrapped in blankets, they huddled for warmth and comfort and spoke in whispers in this threatening sea of English.

They needed each other absolutely, they both knew this, each the other's last hope. There were no words that would shake Rosa from feeling that her daughter's death had been her doing, if only for the fact that the child had died instead of her. He'd known religion in his youth and prayed often as a boy that God would strike down his father. Now he prayed for that same God to ease her suffering. Finally she told him of her first days after being brought ashore and how they'd found shelter that first night in the shell of a building and how, as they wandered the streets looking for food and water, she'd covered her daughter's eyes again and again when they came across bodies burned and twisted. Soon they'd learned to sleep in the open. They'd heard the crash of buildings coming down in the middle of the night, like the dull roll of thunder a street over. They drank what water they could find, drawn up from the Thames, and when the dysentery came it found her daughter quickly, weakened as she was. After she died her mother sat with her for a full day trying to understand why she should not take her own life, then carried her to the pyres.

NOW, IN THE MONTHS leading into winter, a small city of tents and work stations grew up around the Parish Church as more evacuees arrived. They came by truck and car and on foot, the blind and the sighted, the hungry and half-frozen, all drawn by faint hope and the need to escape the pestilence and starvation and desperate to know that something of England stood beyond the circle of ruins.

BY EARLY DECEMBER SHE knew she was pregnant. She did not share this news with him, half-convinced and hopeful that she'd lose the child naturally. It would be cruel and cowardly of her to bring the pregnancy to term, and so she carried on in her silence, living within the confines of the rope maze that guided the blind through the church and out into the churchyard, where the mess tents and the cleaning stations and the latrines were ever busy. Something would go wrong soon, she hoped, but the pregnancy did not let up, and she knew she'd have to summon the courage to end it by her own hand.

On her way to the latrine one morning she almost tripped over something blocking her path. She reached down and felt along its seat and handlebars and wheels, like a child exploring a Christmas present through heavy wrapping. She moved the bicycle off the path, then she clasped the rope again and continued on.

She came to find it later that day when she understood what she had to do. It was where she'd left it. She crouched and ran her hands over it again, exploring it more carefully. It was beaten up, useless now to anyone but her, the spokes loose and dangling from the wheel rims. She turned and twisted one of the spokes until it gave way and slid it into her sleeve and carried it with her to the latrine. She waited in line, holding the single spoke against her arm. When it was her turn she entered the outhouse and hiked up her dress and leaned back against the clapboard siding and thought of the debts and deprivations the world would claim on a new-born in a place like this. She imagined the misery it would suffer, if it survived at all, and how she could not bear losing a second child. She would never forgive herself if she let it be.

It was better off unborn than murdered or starved to death or taken by disease. This would be the one good act left for her to perform. She prayed for the strength to come as she held the thin sharp spoke in her hand below the raised dress, but her courage failed her that day, and when she finally knew this she straightened her dress and stepped out of the privy, something gone in her heart now, and followed the rope back in the direction of the church.

HE TOOK TO SLEEPING with his hand on her abdomen after she told him what she'd almost done. He understood her. He knew she was right. But on that first night after her confession he felt something rising up from where his hand rested against her warmth. It travelled along the length of his arm and touched his heart. He felt surprised and frightened. He wondered if he hadn't gone mad now with this fire burning in him, feeling something for this doomed child. Rosa was asleep, cowled in her blanket, when he recognized this as the currency of life that it was. It came to him as if discovered for the first time, wholly and perfectly new and alive. This was their hope and future, the one best reason to push on.

Teams arrived to begin processing evacuees to be boarded on transport ships bound for India, Australia, Canada, and South Africa. The blind and the sick were of no use to anyone here. Berlin wanted them gone, rotten and dying as they were. Repurposed cargo ships, steamers, and clippers from across the Commonwealth put in at ports along England's southeast coast, and in early April, Georg Elser and Rosa Bauer boarded the hospital ship *Llandovery Castle* at Barrier Gardens Pier and embarked on the journey that would finally deliver them to Mercy House on the other side of the Atlantic.

1960

The punishments meted out to me for leaving the bench without permission after my strapping went on for the rest of that school year. I didn't tell my parents about it. Thomas did what he could for me during recess, but these battles were mine. He had his own to fight, and we were helpless against Principal Crouse's hatred of me. I was to be made an example of whenever and wherever the opportunity arose, which it did almost every day in the schoolyard. The yard monitors looked away when the bullies came for me for their fair share of retribution, taking it again and again, to the point that I believed I had nothing left to give.

On one of the few afternoons I was spared that spring— this was two weeks or so after the strapping—I entered the drugstore on Main Street, gloomy and fearful as I often was, hoping to disappear into the fantasy of *Doctor Atom* for but a few moments to help forget the torment that followed me around all day.

Three schoolboys entered the store. A new bolt of fear shot through me. I moved into the next aisle over to avoid being seen, behind shelves of tinned vegetables and cereal boxes, and overheard them talking about something they called the Rademacher Wave. I didn't know what that was, but I knew the name Rademacher well enough. He was the German foreign minister and architect of the European Clearances whom my father referred to as a venomous reptile. He shook his head in disgust every time he saw that name in the paper or heard it spoken on the radio. He cursed the Red Scare hysteria that made Washington cozy up to a criminal like that. It was a crying shame, he said, to see the way those politician-cowards were willing to shake hands with one devil to keep another devil at bay. Yet as I stood there in ambush that afternoon, fearful that another beating was coming my way, the connection between the foreign minister Rademacher and this "wave" the boys were talking about was still unclear to me.

"They'll be coming over on whatever floats," one of the boys said. "We'll be flooded with 'em—those Jews that'll want to come up here from America before it's too late."

"They'll drown before they get here," another boy said. He turned and saw me through the shelving. "A good number of them, anyway. But that suits you just fine, doesn't it, Teufel? Maybe they should ship all you Krauts over to Africa instead. See how you like it."

Thomas was shooting baskets in the driveway when I got home five minutes later. I'd come as fast as I could, convinced I needed to tell him right away what I'd heard. But he didn't react as I'd thought he would. Instead a smile grew over his face, as if he'd just learned there was ice cream for dessert today. He sank a free shot and captured the ball and put it under his arm. I asked him if he wasn't afraid. He smiled and attempted another basket, this one missing.

The films we'd watched in history class showed railcars being loaded with Jews and travelling over vast European flats, and later cargo ships on the voyage through the Suez to the Red Sea and the Indian Ocean. Our teachers made sure we understood the European Clearances for what they were and not as they'd been represented in the German propaganda of the time. It was the forced deportation of a people and not the settling of a colony in Madagascar, the island nation off Portuguese Guinea. Afterwards, the teacher in charge of these films liked to direct his questions at me and the two other German boys in class. Do you see what your people have done, Mr. Koehler? Can it be any clearer than this, Mr. Heilbronn? Perhaps you have something to say, Mr. Teufel? Unable to speak, we hung our heads in shame.

Once, as my family and I watched the latest Hitchcock at the Playhouse on Main Street, the projector jammed and the film seemed to melt on the screen before our very eyes just as Eva Marie Saint passed the stolen German nuclear codes to the British agent in Sydney. The audience began to protest, calling for the projectionist to save the moment or to go hang himself. It was a lively group. We'd all been looking forward to seeing those nuclear codes being turned against Berlin. The projectionist put on an old *The World in Action* reel—the first thing to come to hand, I suppose—while he tried to fix the problem. These reels had been common enough years earlier but were no longer shown. This one, a short by Leni Riefenstahl, jumped to life before us.

We saw smiling families—played by actors, my father told us later—escorted from their battered homes to the safety of modern trains and passenger liners that carried them to the glittering shores of the new Eretz Israel. I saw the name of the ship when the camera panned its length. It was the *St. Louis*, the one that had carried my mother to the Azores. When the shot cut from the bow to the upper decks, where men and women lounged and played badminton and children skipped rope, my father stood abruptly and announced that we were leaving.

This was nothing but filthy propaganda, he said. He helped my mother into the aisle and marched his sons in the direction of the lobby. As he did so I managed one last look over my shoulder and saw travellers, wearing expressions of gratitude and joy, descending a gangplank as they were received into the heart of the new Jewish Homeland.

We found the manager in his small office just off the lobby. My father threatened to report the man and his cinema to the authorities for showing the garbage we'd just seen. The manager, unaware of what his projectionist had done, practically tripped over himself as he bolted from the lobby and up the narrow set of stairs to the projection room. I don't know if my father ever did report the infraction, but the Playhouse continued to operate after that. We never returned as a family. The point wasn't lost on me. The truth could be told in different ways. I understood my father's outrage. What had been an ugly and vicious reality had been portrayed as the exact opposite. Families delivered to a land of bright sunlight and widened opportunity. He made sure as we walked home that evening to tell me and Thomas the truth about the European Clearances, already more than a million souls displaced and housed in camps that made Little Berlin, north of our town, look like a playground.

Now, with America planning a similar clearance, my brother seemed unfazed. He took this news with a calm shrug, basketball in hand, then sank another free shot.

"Swish," he said.

I tried to grab the ball as it landed. He was too fast for me.

"Jesus Christ," I said, eager to make myself understood, but our mother tapped at the window overlooking the driveway right then and waved us in.

I wanted to tell my parents what I knew but I was afraid this would upset my mother, just as that strapping had upset her.

It was well into the evening, after my father had beaten

me in chess three games in a row, that I found Thomas down at the lake, standing ankle-deep in the water as he stared at the horizon. His shoes and socks were up on the stone beach, neatly side by side. The light was tinged with a soft evening glow that made the world seem much more peaceful than it really was, the glint coming off the water shimmering against his legs and face. Over Hamilton the sky burned the deep red and yellow of the smelters and blast furnaces that would throw their light higher and deeper as dark fell.

I wondered if he hadn't understood what I'd told him.

We'd be flooded with refugees before the summer was out, that's how bad it was over there, I said. Again, he met my disbelief with a smile.

"And that's where you're wrong, little brother," he said finally, reaching into the water for a stone. He skipped it over the surface. "What do you think's going to happen when everyone at school finds out that the Teufel brothers rescued a boatful of God's chosen?" The stone sank after its fifth skip.

I shrugged.

"The Devil brothers become angels. We'll be heroes. No one'll ever bother us ever again."

OUR FOCUS ON MERCY House blurred in the following weeks as we prepared to receive the wave of Jewish refugees we expected to be washing ashore from America any day now. They would be safe in the sanctuary states that had been established after the Secessionist Crisis gripped that country at the end of the war. But the strip of land we saw from here was sanctuary to no one. The counties of northwestern New York—Niagara, Orleans, Monroe, and Wayne—had accepted the executive order that would remove the Jewish population from the U.S. economy. Cities and counties in states from California to Maine had rejected the Decree for the Reporting of Jewish-Owned Property, but too many had chosen to walk in lock-step with President Thurmond, who kept a residence outside Berlin and spoke often of his dream of returning America to its former glory.

We visited the lake as often as we could after devising our plan, stashing various supplies we might need—a flashlight and length of rope, blankets, a bag of candy bars and apples—refreshing the perishables every few days. Drinking water was hidden in three different locations. We had maps to offer our new friends by which they'd situate themselves on this foreign shore. On them we'd drawn a red *X* over our town and a straight line charting the forty-two miles between here and Wilson Beach, New York, which we thought would be the likely launching point of the fugitives we'd receive. We sketched out the steps we'd follow once we got our refugees safely to shore. We'd deliver them to our home, where our mother would provide them with immediate care, if required, and from there we'd make the telephone calls that would bring the authorities and newspaper reporters who'd spread word of our good deed. It would all go according to plan if we stuck to it, which we believed we'd be diligent and thorough enough to do.

Into the first week of our vigil a small party of Jews was rescued near Kingston, fifty miles east, helped to shore by a man who'd been tossing sticks into the lake for his dog on a Sunday morning. The paper showed the newcomers smiling grimly for the camera on the front steps of a local hospital hours after coming to shore, not quite starved after four days on the lake but dehydrated, weary, and relieved. They spoke to the *Whig-Standard* of the roving gangs that visited certain neighbourhoods in Rochester carrying baseball bats and axes, and of the rising anti-Semitism that grew from the decrees of an increasingly nervous and xenophobic White House.

Two days later three rafts were towed to shore near the Scarborough Bluffs, closer to us but still too far west for a couple of kids on bikes to do anything about it. The outer edge of the Rademacher Wave seemed intent on landing everywhere but where we needed it to. We didn't give up hope, though. We fuelled our waiting with fantasies and daydreaming. Our mission would be compared to the one that had rescued fugitive slaves travelling via the Underground Railroad a hundred years earlier. Instead of 169061-4 painted on our front door there'd be a plaque bearing our family name in honour of our good work.

The stretch of shoreline we focused on was practically as

familiar to us as our own backyard. It became more familiar still as we moved into the early days of that summer. We'd been exploring and skipping stones and building driftwood forts there for as long as I could remember. We didn't go to Mercy House anymore but, like a stubborn memory, it was never far, often visible, and always no more than a short walk from where we scoured our shoreline.

In previous summers the lakeshore had never failed to provide something that occupied us for hours at a time—a carp rotting at water's edge; the dead sheep we'd studied for days with undiminished pleasure as it succumbed to the heaving mass of maggots that colonized its hollowed shell; we'd found a man's wallet once, emptied; a broken baby carriage; and, unaccountably, a length of rope tied in a hangman's noose. There was a long line of single shoes, broken umbrellas, deflated soccer and beach balls; a life jacket; buoys and bottles; and even once a ray-gun, its plastic yellow-and-red handle tinged with green algae. One summer we'd spent days scraping fool's gold from the rocks at the bottom of Jones Avenue. In winter we'd jumped onto an ice floe in the shallow bay, almost floating out into open lake before we managed to paddle back to shore using the hockey sticks we'd carried with us.

Now we looked to the horizon and not down at our feet as we ranged between the harbour to the west and the seawall to the east, a good mile or so, which felt ten times that due to the rocks and boulders we scaled. We often went down there at night, too, in pitch-dark but for the stars and the red glow from the Stelco plant that brushed the western sky. It didn't matter how well you knew the terrain at night, it was treacherous and irregular—a miracle one of us or both didn't break a leg or at least turn an ankle. But down we went during the day and at night, more and more as the weather warmed and finally school let out for the summer. My punishments had continued till the last day. By now, more than ever, it was clear to me that this plan we'd devised needed to work. It was the only way I'd survive the coming school year.

Our request to sleep on the back deck was refused that evening. We waited, conspiring, and once our parents were settled in bed, we snuck out through the upstairs bathroom window and retrieved our bicycles from the garage and coasted to the bottom of Sanctuary Road, where we stashed our bikes and assumed our lookout on the old limestone pier built by American militiamen captured by the British during the War of 1812—the first time in our history when the Royal Navy ruled the Great Lakes—and waited and watched and dreamed. The lake at this late hour was usually as still as glass, and the moon when it showed itself traced a beam as white as snow over the water. Always there was the glow of the steel plant in the west.

On those evenings we were allowed to sleep on the back deck we listened to our neighbours' television sets and the barking dogs that sometimes chased us down our street. We took long sips of water that later obliged us to sneak out to the edge of the garden to relieve ourselves. Sometimes we talked about what our lives might be like if our mother wasn't German. It was a pleasant thought to imagine her as an Australian or Norwegian or South African. There would be no number painted on our door and no bonfires in the front yard. Our father's half-German parentage would mean little, and Thomas and I would be known as the Norwegian brothers, or whatever other harmless bloodline, and we would be free and clean and unremarkable. But she was German, and no amount of fantasizing could change that fact. I felt disloyal for wishing that she was someone else, and I wondered too if I would treat people like us the way we ourselves were treated if our father had married a woman who did not bear a shameful heritage. But this would not matter much longer, for we were upon that summer of our changing luck—our time had come—and I'd walk out over the lawn in my bare feet to the edge of the garden where I'd pee in the grass while Thomas, who never tired of pestering me, taunted my privacy with his flashlight beam.

One evening in early July we prepared for a late-night visit to the lake, as we usually did, by telling our mother once again of our intention to sleep out back. She helped me with our sleeping bags and pillows while Thomas fetched his flashlight. We waited until our parents' room fell dark— we could see the window from where we lay on the deck— and gave ourselves another twenty minutes for them to fall asleep, then crept off to see if we'd find any newly arrived refugees camped out on the lakeshore.

The neighbourhood was quiet, as it usually was at this hour, close to midnight—the houses up and down Douglas Avenue dark and lonely-looking. The problem dogs were chained and silent now, and not a soul stirred but us. In the weeks since we'd taken up our vigil we'd seen no pedestrians or traffic pass on Main Street, which lay between our house and the lake, and no sign of the Citizen Patrol we knew to look out for. This fact had always given me the feeling that our mission had been blessed in some vague and unconfirmable way.

As we prepared to cross that night we saw headlights coming towards us from the east. We got behind a hedge next to a street lamp and waited for the vehicles to pass. There were three in all, the same sort of transports the scientists used on inspection day. I saw the labourers crammed in the back as the first one drove past. These were the men who paved roads and dug ditches and picked our fruit. Now they were on their way home to one of the internment camps an hour northwest, in Grand Valley near Orangeville, or farther still, near Kitchener. Or maybe even just up the road to Little Berlin. The second and third trucks passed in quick succession. The back flap of each was open and snapping in the wind. As the last truck passed us one of the men inside turned his head in our direction and seemed to hold on us, as if studying our faces.

We stayed at the lake longer than usual that night, talking about how close we ourselves had come to the life most Germans in Canada were living in those days. It was close to one o'clock when we got home. The house was dark. We snuck up the driveway and came through the garage into the backyard and slipped into our sleeping bags. They were damp and cold. We watched the stars while we waited to warm up, and we finally went upstairs to our room and got into our beds.

WE ACCOMPANIED OUR FATHER to the shipyard the next morning. He knew nothing about our nightly excursions, it seemed, and until that day I'd felt no qualms or guilt in keeping this secret from him. We were always afraid of being caught by our parents, or worse, by the neighbourhood patrol. But stronger than this was the hope that we'd be able to offer this gift to our mother and father, and to ourselves. It would be a marvellous surprise when we notified them of the rescue we'd effect and the subsequent praise that would free us from our troubles. But now, after being spotted by one of the men in the convoy, we feared that our secret would be discovered, and that someone would come to our house to question us. We'd always been careful to keep to the shadows, but we could never be sure that this project of ours was known only to us.

My father noticed the dark circles under my eyes. He asked

if sleeping out there on the back deck was such a good idea and was something wrong? He didn't recognize the lie when I shook my head. He placed a hand on my shoulder and kept it there as we walked. He was responding to me on a simpler level than I needed then, as a father does with a son who's lost some small struggle that he will naturally rise up from again, like heartache or a betrayal of friendship, but the truth of the matter was more complicated than anything I understood.

On our way back from the shipyard, Thomas and I crossed the bridge via the catwalk. It was a sort of steel-mesh walkway on the underside of the bridge that seemed to disappear underfoot, the grating so coarse and open that you could see the river far below. Parallel to the catwalk was the heavy under-structure of deck-plates and crossbeams that were now home to a large colony of pigeons breeding and nesting with their young. We'd heard about them on the news. It was a breed of pigeon, called rock doves, that you couldn't find in all of England, hunted as they'd been by an occupied population that had turned to eating its horses, dogs, and cats already years before. Here there were hundreds of these birds nesting in the trestlework, a selfish abundance, it seemed to me. They watched us, exercising their beautiful blue-and-grey wings in sudden bursts.

Reported with righteous indignation, the food crisis in England was in the news often. Every fall and spring, students from our school fanned out through town to canvass for money, clothing, and tinned goods, the latter two of which we piled high on the gymnasium floor over a period of weeks, then crated and sent it over. The whole country participated in those clothing and food drives back then. We were never sure that the things we sent over didn't end up in Germany. We knew of the import taxes imposed on these charitable contributions, which was the nomenclature the German bureaucrats chose to apply to their theft. As we stood there on the catwalk watching the horizon I wondered if we shouldn't capture the pigeons that surrounded us and send them over to England.

"It tastes like chicken, anyway," Thomas said, removing the blue plastic straw he'd been carrying behind his ear that day.

Our mother knew what it was like to feel real hunger. She'd told us more than once that it didn't matter what something tasted like, food was food. She'd learned this well enough in the camp in the Azores. I didn't like the idea of eating pigeon meat. It seemed cruel to me. I didn't think I could harm a single one of those birds, not even if I was starving, after watching the way they ran their beaks through their feathers and puffed and preened themselves.

Thomas loaded an unlit match into one end of his straw and leaned forward over the railing with his peashooter held to his pursed lips. He concentrated his aim and blew as hard as he could. The match head ignited when it struck the iron beam a few inches above one of the pigeons. It dropped harmlessly into the nest. He had a full box of matches to shoot. He tried again, aiming each time as if that match were his last.

Every so often he flicked out the saliva that accumulated in the straw, and then he redoubled his efforts. Some of the match heads failed to ignite when they struck the ironwork, but most of them flared and dropped their bright flame into the nests below, only to gutter out and disappear. I didn't like what he was doing. I told him to stop. He kept on shooting those matches, most of them flaring and dropping uselessly into or near a nest, until there were no more matches left, and we continued on over to the far side of the bridge, climbed up onto the road using the utility ladder we'd discovered there, and made for home.

IN PREVIOUS SUMMERS WE'D often visited the abandoned fallout shelters around our neighbourhood. We enjoyed exploring their damp, cool spaces. We thought of them as forts, places we deemed our own. We weren't able to gain entry into the shelters that the town still maintained for their original purpose—those were locked and serviced by the air-raid wardens you still saw occasionally climbing on one of the sirens, his loose tool belt slapping against his thigh. The shelters we called in on had been taken over by raccoons and the vagrants who haunted our town.

They were easy enough to break into. As I say, we'd not visited any so far that year, and on the Saturday in early June when we pushed through the warped plywood barring the entrance of the shelter on Randall Street we were met by a wall of stale air, the light as thin and tired as we'd always known it. The walls of the shelter were flaking and crumbled to the touch now, almost sixteen years after their construction. Our father had told us that the engineers who'd managed the building of these shelters had been forced to use a grade of cement inferior to the type used in the construction of the Miracle Canal due to shortages and priority rationing, and so it was natural for them to fall apart as quickly as they did.

No one ever really thought the duck-and-cover drills we were made to practise once a month at school would do much good in the event of a full-on nuclear exchange, especially after seeing the film reels that showed the horror of London. A shelter like this might save your life, though. The intermittent blaring of an air-raid siren was a regular feature of life in those days, and we knew what to do if that short staccato blast rolled into the long, constant droning that was not a test.

The shelter we chose that afternoon was set back in an empty lot just off the street. A plywood sheet made an improvised door that you could see from the sidewalk, and the shelter itself travelled fifty or so feet under the low hill that rose to the adjacent street the next block over.

We cut across the field and wrenched open the loose plywood and descended the concrete steps. Thomas struck one of the matches he had with him that day—he always carried matches, in case we found a package that still had one or two unsmoked cigarettes in it, and to bombard the helpless pigeons nested under the bridge with—and turned in a slow circle and whistled. I told him there'd be no echo here, it was too small, and he said he was whistling for hobos, not echoes—he just wanted to let them know we were here. You wouldn't want to surprise a hobo out of his sleep, would you? he said. You had to be careful with their lot, what with the knives and diseases they carried.

The space was as long and wide as a school bus. There were benches along the lengths of the walls and a small cabinet, empty now, that might have contained medical supplies and provisions. The ceiling was low and there were smaller, locked doors that led off to who-knew-where.

"Everyone in here would burn like a marshmallow if there was ever a war," Thomas said. "They put these here just to make you feel safe—just like those fake reports after the inspectors leave."

"Even this deep?" I said. We might have been fifteen feet underground. I'd believed what we'd always been told about the effectiveness of these shelters.

"From the detonation, maybe, if it's far enough away," he said. "Like Toronto or Hamilton. But the radiation creeps into your bones and melts you from inside. Just like those people down at Blind Man's Alley." He swore and dropped the match when the flame touched his fingers. "And the bombs are stronger than they were. These shelters were built for 1944 bombs. They were nothing compared to now."

MY FATHER HAD A worried expression on his face when he got home from work that afternoon. He didn't ask us about our day or tousle my hair the way he often did. He sat at the kitchen table holding a full glass of water and watched our mother working at the kitchen sink. There was something going on between them. I took an apple from the fruit bowl beside the fridge and sat down and ate it. After a time he got up and crossed the kitchen and turned down the stove and said he needed to see her upstairs. They did this when there was something important to talk about. On one occasion they'd shut themselves in their bedroom to discuss an issue, and when my mother came back downstairs her eyes were red and puffy, and my father walked nervously about the house for the rest of the evening. I had no doubt that they'd convened to speak about us slipping out of the house in the middle of the night. One or both of them had heard us, I thought, and they'd let us know that our lies would not go unpunished.

After a short time in their bedroom my mother, dry-eyed as if nothing had happened, came back downstairs, and my father shut himself in the bathroom to scrub away the day's work the way he usually did. When he was finished he sat on the front steps and watched Thomas and me kick the soccer ball around in the field across the street. I'd cleared out of the house to tell my brother that something was going on between our mom and dad. I said I thought they knew what we'd been up to. They didn't know a thing about it, he said. I tried to act as if I wasn't worried. From across the way I couldn't see the expression on my father's face as he sat on the steps, but more and more it was clear that something was wrong. He went back inside twice, returning again to sit and shake his head, as if to say that nothing of this made any sense to him.

He was wearing a fresh white T-shirt and grey slacks that afternoon. I smelled only the grass beneath our feet and the early summer and the vague tang of the lake three blocks south, but I knew he'd be wearing the light cologne he liked to put on after his bath and shaving. There was a time, not so long before then, when I would often soap and scrub his back as he sat in the tub, and afterwards watch him shave his face with the heavy flair-tip razor that opened like a claw. As he carved the white lather from his chin and sideburns and upper lip he liked to tell me about the crane he operated at the shipyard, or the flame-cutter that parted two-inch steel like butter, or how sometimes he climbed Tarzan-like on the ten-storey maze of scaffolding that encased a ship as it grew in its various stages of construction. These were wonderful things to hear. The names of the machines and tools he talked about thrilled me, though half the time I didn't know what these things were supposed to do. It was a mark of his confidence in me that he spoke of come-alongs, shackles, and hydraulic cylinders as easily as he did, and I was content to accept the secret function of these devices as a mystery better left unsolved.

Now, he sat on the front porch steps shaking his head in what appeared to be disbelief or disgust. I had no idea what was coming. I wondered if I'd be able to tell the lie my brother wanted me to tell—that we'd not left the house last night or seen the convoy of interned labourers. We passed the ball back and forth between us, doing our best to pretend all was well, and finally our father got up and crossed the street and intercepted the ball we'd been kicking. He'd just turned forty that spring, still healthy, with the thick head of dark hair that fell over his eyes when he leaned forward. He was a fit and handsome man and better with a soccer ball than either me or my brother. He flicked it up and held it under his arm and stared at us, waiting. I caught a whiff of his cologne. It was sweet and foreign-smelling, the one my mother said she liked best. I wondered if he'd put it on for her that afternoon.

His eyes were sharp and focused with worry. He was the sort of man who was willing to defend his home and family with a baseball bat, but could also appear to be as unsure and halting as he now seemed to me.

"Have you spoken to your mother yet?" he said.

The dread that had taken me subsided a little then. He was usually the one who dealt with the necessities of discipline in our family. If our mother needed to speak to us, perhaps the chosen course of action would be less than the strapping I felt coming. There might only be a lecture on the way, and some sort of grounding. She was softer on us when it came to this sort of thing, and I was pleased to think that it was her call.

"About what?" Thomas said.

"Your mother has some news for you both."

His mood, sad until now, seemed to shift to a state of agitation. His jaw tensed and he motioned in the direction of the house with a tough jerk of his head. We followed him, soccer ball in hand, which we left on the porch, and found her setting the table in the falling light of our kitchen.

Her eyes were not red, which would have meant she'd been crying, but she looked different to me, ready for something, purposely composed. She straightened her apron and smiled when we came in. I couldn't think of anything he'd be so disturbed or saddened by if it hadn't bothered her in the same way it had him. My thoughts went to the death of a relative. We'd not seen our father's parents in over a year— the three-hour drive to their town was difficult, the rationed gasoline hard to come by and too expensive on the black market—but certainly such a task would fall to him, not her. I supposed her brother back in Germany might be the issue. But she didn't look upset. And no mail had come from Germany in months. There was no phone service between here and Europe, not for the likes of us. A telegram might have come, but, as I say, she didn't look upset or emotional in a way that would lead you to think she'd heard any bad news.

The potatoes she'd prepared sent clouds of steam rising from the bottom of the sink. The steam fogging up the window revealed the happy face, now revived, though more obliquely, that I'd drawn on the window in better times.

"Go on, then, tell them," he said. "Tell them your wonderful plans."

Sarcasm was not used in our house. It did not suit him one bit. It wasn't the father I knew who'd speak like that. But what surprised me more was the fact that this rudeness did not give her pause. She met the taunt with an indifference that shocked and then, in a moment, pleased me, not for its own sake but for the fact that she would bring this odd tension between them to rest by not letting it affect her in the least.

"Something good's happened, boys. Come, sit," she said. "I'm just trying to help your father understand. A blessing's fallen at our feet."

Thomas and I looked at each other, puzzled. Our father remained standing.

"I'm going home." She repeated this in German, then smiled and opened her hands, like a magician releasing an invisible dove.

"Only be for a short visit," she said, switching back into English. "You won't even notice I'm gone, you two running around wild all day the way you do."

She began to ladle out our supper, first to our father's plate, then Thomas's and mine, and lastly to her own.

"Your father doesn't think it's such a good idea," she said. "You can see that. I think I've made a worrywart of him. Is that the word—worrywart?"

He'd made our kitchen table and chairs two or three years earlier. For a month the garage had smelled of white pine and glue. The chairs were stained a light-gold colour and bore the sort of German motifs that our mother stitched into the clothes she sewed for us. He'd cut the shape of a heart into the backrest of each chair roughly the size of what might have been an actual human heart, and now as he stared at his wife, our plates steaming with potatoes, he gripped the back of his chair through that cut-out heart and said he would not allow it.

"You can't trust those people to hold to this—this *amnesty*," he said. "It's propaganda. Just a lie."

It was the word Toby Schwabe had used, of course. But now it was much bigger than a schoolyard disagreement. The lie threatened something that still bound my parents together—trust or goodwill or maybe something as simple as common sense.

They didn't budge from their positions that evening as we ate our supper. It was a tense, brief meal, and afterwards they sought out opposite sides of the house.

I sat in the backyard and played chess with my father. He was not so concentrated on our games as usual. I won two out of three, something that had never happened before. He didn't say much, and after the third game he said he was going to work in the garden for a bit. This was something he did when he wanted to be alone.

I found my mother sitting on the porch steps around front, an unfinished and as yet undefinable piece of clothing growing inch by inch from the tips of the needles that clacked away between her fingers. It was the soft, repetitive nature of this work that comforted her, as it did me. She seemed peaceful and almost happy now, though I didn't know how that could be after what she'd proposed only an hour or so earlier.

She nodded and smiled without speaking when I sat down beside her. The last of the day was fading, leaving behind its dash of orange in the sky. The colours playing on the field across the road deepened from purple and brown to a thick, sombre grey. She told me that all this would make sense one day. It might not now but it would. She said I'd look back and understand everything, maybe once I'd grown up and had a family of my own, and that sometimes people have to leave behind certain ideals they'd thought they would carry with them forever. I didn't know what she was talking about. She used that word, *ideals*. It was an unusual word for her to use, in German or in English. I thought she was trying to communicate something to me about what happens when you're married and about parents having disagreements and fighting sometimes. And then it was dark and we sat there for a while longer, me feeling unsure, but proud that my mother had spoken to me in this way, like I was old enough to understand about mothers and fathers, though I don't think I was, and then with not enough light left in the sky to knit anymore we got up and went back inside.

THAT NIGHT OUR FATHER sat at the edge of my bed and tried to convince us that we had nothing to worry about. "Your mother's not going anywhere," he said. It was the nostalgia she was prone to, he said. He'd probably be the same too if the shoe were on the other foot. We couldn't blame her for missing her people back there. Her brother, at least. He paused for a moment. But it was an impossible country to go back to because the place she remembered wasn't there anymore, he told us. The war had changed everything. There and here, he said. She was just having a hard time believing that.

I wanted her to appear at the door then and nod silently, or maybe sit with us and say that things were going to get better soon. But she didn't come and sit with us that night, and our father couldn't think of anything else to say. He sat with us a little while longer, which was something he used to do when we were younger and there wasn't the need to explain so much to us. Then he leaned forward and kissed us each on the forehead and left the room.

MY MOTHER'S PARENTS HAD died since she'd come to Canada, but she had a younger brother back there who'd missed serving in the war by only a few years. He worked at the Bavarian Broadcasting Corporation now as a cultural liaison officer between Germany and America. A letter came from him perhaps once a year. It was fascinating to watch my mother read these. Sitting opposite her, I'd see her face through the holes in the airmail paper where a censor had cut away a line here and there. I never asked where the cutting had been done, there or here, or what secrets between a brother and sister the person with the scissors was looking for. She'd sent at least as many to Munich, where he lived, and I imagined those light blue sheets of paper she so painstakingly wrote on snipped to a fragile fish-bone skeleton falling to pieces in her brother's hand.

Once we heard a documentary he'd worked on, broadcast from one of the dozen or so floating pirate radio stations on the fleet of ships dedicated to that purpose sailing the American side of the Great Lakes, aiming their propaganda into the heart of what they liked to call the "crumbling socialist commonwealth." This was somewhere around 1956 or '57 when the America First Committee started using radio and television to reach into the homes of millions of Americans and, more and more, into Canadian homes. I remember that evening clearly. I was eight or nine. My father was against it—tuning into that radio station. It was well known that doing so was prohibited and could lead to problems. They might cut your gasoline rations or your family food stamp quotas if they found out. But this was family, after all, my mother argued. We'd listen not for whatever politics it might bring but for a familiar voice, a blood connection. She'd not heard her brother's voice in fifteen or more years by this point. My father finally relented.

I felt a thrill of anticipation when we heard the signal come through that evening, faint and crackling from the storm that troubled the airwaves over the lake. Outside, sheets of rain beat against our living room window. My mother adjusted the dial, hoping for better reception. There were evenings when a signal came clear—others not at all. Sometimes it would drift from a regular station and suddenly, without us realizing at first, we'd be listening to the voice of the American poet Ezra Pound, who hosted a program called *Nations Arise* and spoke of the record of Hebrew barbarism and the lies of the British government-in-exile and the imminent annexation of Canada, Newfoundland, and Jamaica. There were other American stations and programs that weren't jammed by the authorities. WNEB played *Family Theatre*, *The Adventures of Sam Spade*, and *The Bing Crosby Show*. WYRK had *Perry Mason* and the Western series called *Red Ryder*. My favourite was the *Suspense Radio Theatre* with Vincent Price, whose movies we saw on Main Street, as I said. I liked his voice and the way the music and the sound effects rose and fell in the background when he spoke.

But that evening the signal came clear enough to make out what was being said, crackly and distant but it was there, and my mother's face lit up when her brother's voice rose from the speaker. He did not sound like her, of course, but in my child's mind I almost expected him to. She took hold of my hand and squeezed when he spoke. This program, called *The White Honour Hour*, told stories in English and

German from and about the Fatherland. He spoke in that smooth rich tenor that radio men used in those days and asked the many tens of thousands of German-Canadians repressed under Soviet-British rule if they were now ready to rise in whatever fashion they could. Strikes. Civil unrest. Even sabotage. The German people must free themselves from the socialist tyranny of colonial rule, he said.

My father leaned forward and switched off the radio. The glow of the set flickered to darkness. It was one of the only times I saw my father visibly angry. He swore under his breath and stared at her, and then barked at us to get to bed. I heard them arguing from where I lay under my covers. It was a terrible thing to hear. I tried to sleep but couldn't. Later I went to the stairs and saw my mother seated in the chair by the green lamp, her knitting needles in her hands. The storm outside had stopped now. I heard the sound of dripping against a windowsill. She didn't move a muscle. My father was nowhere to be seen. Maybe he was out walking, trying to clear his head. My mother didn't move as she sat there, her eyes closed, thinking what, I'll never know.

WE SAW THE CONVOY of trucks pass through town close to midnight for a second time in three days after our mother announced her intention to go home. We stood behind the same hedge we had that first night and watched them rumble past. But this time Thomas stepped clear of the hedge and into the cone of light that came down from the overhead street lamp just as the last truck went past. He was eager to get to the lake where we might resume our vigil, I thought. But that wasn't it. That's not why he stepped out onto the curb. He wanted those men to see him. I had no idea what he was up to until he raised his right hand and gave the same salute the boys in the school hallway had mocked me with. He threw them a *Sieg Heil* like it was Göring himself in that last truck. He stood in the cone of light that fell from the street lamp, his arm unwavering, the lights of the trucks fading as they continued down Main Street. Our father had always talked about the importance of letting the town know that we were on the right side. That's why we went as a family to the memorial services at Chisolm Square every August. That's why he worked at the shipbuilding yard. That's why we tolerated the fires on our front lawn when Remembrance Day came. It was clear now that my brother had made up his own mind about whose side he was on, and from that night onwards I waited with terror in my heart for men to come to our door with the eviction orders that would send us away.

I KEPT MY DISTANCE for the next few days while I watched him, hoping for a sign that the salute was no more than a reckless impulse he now felt ashamed of. I listened for the sort of slurs and innuendo Toby had brought to me in the schoolyard a few months earlier but heard none. I'd confronted Thomas the evening of the salute as we stood on the beach, waiting for a sign of the Jewish refugees we thought would be coming ashore any time now. He shrugged at first and said nothing. I asked again what he was up to, why he'd done something like that. We could be forced from our house, I reminded him. We'd be broken up as a family. It was the stupidest thing he'd ever done. The lake was flat and quiet that night and I was filled with an overwhelming sense of dread, afraid the neighbourhood patrol was already on their way down here to pick us up. Maybe the salute had been seen by someone from their bedroom window. It was on Main Street this had happened, after all, and chances were not remote in the least that someone had seen us. I told him he couldn't do anything like that ever again. He just stared out at the lake while I said my piece, and then he swore and told me he was sick of living like this, always the bad guy. Everyone watching every move. He bent down and picked up a stone and threw it with a great heave as far as he could.

"Maybe we're on the wrong side here," he said. "Maybe we shouldn't believe everything they tell us."

BUT I DID BELIEVE everything, and the fear of our imminent roundup grew the following day. In my mind, it was all but guaranteed. We'd be packed up and shipped off like baggage. I worried through that morning and afternoon as our own personal Doomsday Clock ticked closer to midnight.

Was there any difference between my brother and Toby, I wondered, the boy I'd eagerly reported to the yard monitor when he spoke his lies? I knew I should report my brother for the salute, and for what he'd said, and wondered if, by reporting him, I'd be able to save the rest of my family. I knew enough about Little Berlin to understand we'd suffer there like we'd never suffered before. Even worse was the possibility of being sent to one of the internment camps around the province or far out west.

I didn't sleep much that week. Every night I stared up at the model planes suspended from our bedroom ceiling and imagined shooting down my brother. I wondered if I'd have the courage to do that if I knew he was going to drop a bomb on a village below. Wasn't this the same thing? Sacrificing a loved one for what was right. Our troubles were coming fast and thick now. I knew what a licking he'd get from our father if I told him about that salute, impulse or no impulse, and from then on the resulting doubt and disappointment would always hang between my father and brother.

Added to this, our mother was talking about the amnesty that'd just been announced from Berlin—the *real* Berlin, Thomas said later with a note of satisfaction—and Ottawa had declared that those with relatives in Germany might apply for the required transit visa. These would be expedited upon request. My father insisted it was a ruse on the part of both governments: Ottawa would seize the opportunity to identify sympathizers; and Berlin, which my father had more than once referred to as "the great Sodom, that lost and wicked capital," would always know to take advantage where advantage could be gained. It was propaganda, he said, meant to beguile the willing fools among us.

I didn't blame her for wanting to go back, but nor was I able to understand or forgive her this pull that drew her away from us. It would be natural to want to see your people after so long, but at the same time my small selfish heart felt the betrayal.

I was frightened, too, that she'd entrusted me with that secret as we'd sat together on the front steps a week or so earlier, though its full meaning was lost on me. What was it that I'd eventually understand? What knowledge waited for me on the far side of my youth? It'd sounded as though she'd made up her mind to go, and that one day I'd finally see what had made her do what she did, though at the time I did not know the full scope of her plans.

AFTER THAT WE DIDN'T sleep on the back deck the way we'd been doing up until then. We stopped entirely. Now every night as I lay in bed I pushed away thoughts of life rafts crammed with refugees. Now there was something more urgent and pressing about our home life that pushed those other thoughts away. I tried to ignore the silent tension that was building between our parents, despite the fact that it seemed my father's arguments had won the day—that my mother would be a willing fool to accept the amnesty offer. It seemed she'd dropped the matter, but an unease hung between them. We ate our suppers in complete silence now. The scraping of knives and forks was the only sound you could hear over the radio. If the evening news brought mention of the amnesty, my father would rise from his heartback chair and turn it off with a hard snap of the dial.

It was weeks before the house returned to what seemed like some version of the normal we'd always known. Yet there was a stiffness between my parents that remained. They focused on us and the food on our plates and the chores we were expected to do around the house and yard. We were used to our father telling stories about his day and whatever ships he was unloading at the shipyard. I still played chess with him almost every evening after supper. The fact that he won nine games out of ten I took as a good sign. It meant he was focused and himself again.

I tried to divide my time fairly between them. Often I sat on the front steps with my mother and listened to her talk about when she was a girl. I liked the memories she shared with me. They were always pleasant, set before or outside the threat of the war that eventually came to push her out of her old life. She'd lived in the countryside where she and her brother took care of their two horses and fed chickens and collected water from the well. They walked to school together, and in summertime they swam in a river that was so cold, even on the hottest July day, that they came out frozen to the bone after only a quick dip. I tried to be the son she wanted me to be. I was still at the age when a boy is ill-defined and protean and eager to take after those he loves. I wanted to know what she was like at my age. I imagined she was just like she was now, fully formed, determined, and independent. I'd seen only one photograph of her from that time. She'd carried it with her when she came here. It showed her with a group of thirty or so girls standing against a stone wall, headmaster to the left, another adult, a teacher, to the right. She stood in the centre beside her best friend, a girl named Silke, whom she hadn't seen now in almost thirty years. On the back of the photograph there was a pencil drawing of a heart pierced through with an arrow and the date 15 Oktober 1927.

ONE NIGHT, A FEW weeks later, Thomas told me he thought our mother was right in wanting to take advantage of the amnesty. He'd go too if he had the chance, he said. I was lying in bed staring up at our model airplanes as they cut across our imaginary sky. He was sitting on his desk, feet on the chair, playing with a rubber band.

"They just treat us like garbage here, anyway," he said. It was no mystery to him why she'd want to go back.

"She won't go back there, not for anything," I said, though I was unsure of these words as I spoke them.

He flicked the rubber band at the model Spitfire that followed in pursuit of the Heinkel bomber, suspended just inches behind its tail. It was like we were up there competing for the same thing—me in the Spitfire and him in the German bomber. He was going to bring chaos and shame to our family unless I stopped him.

A FEW DAYS LATER I rode down to Mercy House and waited for that strange figure to appear in the second-floor window. I wanted some distraction. That thought about shooting down my brother was bothering me. I'd never imagined him as an enemy before, but I wasn't able to shake the idea from my mind. The matted grass under the fruit trees on the estate grounds was still wet with dew that morning. I saw this from where I stood, perched on the fieldstone wall. Bird chatter filled the air. The sun was barely up, and the scene before me might have been beautiful if an ugly truth hadn't been secreted away under that peaceful veneer.

It was shame, of course—not courage—that steeled me. As I started up the lane, a cluster of overgrown crabapple and pear trees to my left, I felt I'd discovered a calling, a purpose, and a release from the troubled thoughts that had ruled my summer.

The doorway was huge, tall enough to ride a horse through, like a medieval castle's. The brass knocker was shaped like a fist. I lifted it and let it fall with a crisp, hollow clap. I stepped back and waited. My fingertips tingled, my heart raced. I wondered if the wild schoolyard stories we'd heard about the place were true—that by simply coming through that gate I'd exposed myself to the radiation that was said to linger there. But wasn't this part of the sacrifice that was required? Hardship, sickness, misery. If I'd learned anything about Mercy House it was that those who worked there might receive the absolution I was after—not the public sort promised and denied my mother, but a personal cleansing that would set my heart at ease.

From the doorstep I saw footpaths cutting through stands of maple and willow trees on the north lawn, and three out-buildings, which I later came to know to be a doctor's consulting room, a gardening shed, and a stone chapel, beside which lay a lonely cemetery of headstones.

I didn't have to knock a second time. The door was opened and before me stood someone who, I later learned, was called Sister Catherine. She stepped back as if surprised when she saw me, a boy instead of, what—a delivery man, or the groundskeeper, wheelbarrow and shovel in tow? She was older than my mother, in her forties, I guessed. Her eyes were almost friendly, though not quite welcoming, either, which offered an unexpected contrast to the dour black of her habit and coif and to the image of the place my mother had instilled in me.

"Good morning," Sister Catherine said. "And who are you?"

I told her I'd come to be of some help if help was needed. She regarded me with a puzzled look.

"And what sort of help would that be?"

I told her I would do anything that was required, though I'd not thought this through to a point where I was able to suggest any specific chore.

"Anything you need. I could pick those pears, maybe," I said, referring to the small cluster of trees I'd passed walking up the lane. It was a clumsy offer.

"They won't be ready for another month yet," she said.

I didn't know how to answer this. It was as if the Ontario harvesting season had revealed me for the fraud I was. She must have seen me struggling.

"Well then, young man, do you know what we do here?"

"Yes."

"And what is that?"

"This is a home for the blind," I said.

"Indeed, it is. And what sort of the blind do we have here?"

"The people who were there on that wicked day," I said, hoping the description might clearly identify my allegiance. The word failed to carry the meaning I'd intended, though. The expression on her face registered what appeared to be a note of suspicion.

"What interest would a boy like you have in coming here if he knew such a thing?"

"To help."

"Nobody wants to help here. Least of all a lad like you."

I didn't know what she'd meant by that—if *lad like you* was more accusation than anything else. Maybe she knew who I was. I couldn't admit the truth, of course. She would close the door in my face if I told her that a German boy wanted to prove that he wasn't like other Germans, for that would require some degree of sympathy or understanding, and despite the smile that had greeted me when the door first opened, I began to feel like the fraud I really was, and that I was testing her patience. Yet I deepened the lie I'd initiated. I told her my grandfather was a Londoner and, as I'd never met him, I felt it was my duty to understand something about the war and to do what I could, trifling as this gesture was.

"Is that so?" Sister Catherine said.

I nodded, already half drowning in the story.

"What's your name, boy?" she said.

"Graham Williams," I mumbled, unable to stop myself.

There was a boy named Graham in my math class, and another in my geography class named William. They were likely enough names.

"Speak up, please."

I repeated the invented name.

"In all the years we've been here I can say you're the first one to come with so much as a hello, let alone a helping hand. I'm not sure if we should feel suspicious or grateful."

I wondered if the mounting weight of these lies began playing over my face. My only saving grace would be if she mistook this guilt and gathering embarrassment for a natural apprehension and expression of the awe you'd feel to stand at the threshold of such a house. I was prepared, I remember, to run off if she attempted to grab me by the shoulder.

"Well then, Mr. Williams, be that as it may. We're not so frightening as to cause you to shake in your boots, are we? Come in, come in. We won't bite."

My fingertips were tingling with nervous energy. My head was spinning. I still had time to declare myself, beg forgiveness, and retreat. She didn't have my real name. She would never see me again. But instead of turning and running, I followed Sister Catherine through a long foyer into a front parlour that might have been bigger than my whole house.

From there I saw a grand staircase rising against the back wall of the parlour and, to left and right, dark-panelled walls covered in paintings. The basket-weave wood flooring was exposed but for the large throw rugs that served as colourful islands on which floated elaborate groupings of furniture—gilt Italianate sofas and chesterfields, antler-rack side tables, leather and brass armchairs, lamps, and footstools. Variations of this pattern were repeated throughout the room. The paintings showed scenes of hunting parties and landscapes and portraits of men dressed in clothing from decades past. There was a fireplace almost as tall as me set into one wall. A collection of oversized pine cones, ceramic bowls, two candelabra, and a large clock were set out on the mantle. Over this was a painting of a white-haired and bearded Saint Joseph cradling an infant. Sister Catherine turned to me and said, "The husband of Mary, our Saint Joseph, and patron of the sick." She crossed herself as she walked. "We'll see what errands we'll find for you. Come now, Mr. Williams, you're dawdling."

At the foot of the staircase sat two folded wheelchairs and a tall blue-and-white vase, in which, in a normal house, you might set your umbrella. It was filled with the sort of canes used by the blind. I'd seen these many times at Chisolm Square on the sixth of August, red and white with a bulb at the bottom like a radish. There were seven canes in all, but so far we'd crossed paths with not a single person here. It was oddly quiet for such a big house, and made to feel larger and gloomier still for the fact that it seemed we two were the only ones in it.

On the second floor Sister Catherine ushered me down a long, narrow hallway to a room overlooking the lake. We were on the west side of the house now. From the window I saw the road from which Thomas and I did our creeping and spying. It looked reassuringly familiar—I was not entirely lost in enemy territory—and I wanted to be down there now going about my usual make-believe, and not here trying to prove something to myself.

This room wasn't nearly as large as the one downstairs. Against one wall were a sofa and another small table. The room felt old and slightly shabby, past its time. Two of the walls were lined with books, these ones mostly of a religious nature, if a first glance could be trusted. On a third wall were hung more paintings, smaller than the ones downstairs, three of which depicted schooners tossed on rough seas; the fourth wall was mostly window, its green muntins and rails chipped and flaking.

Out on the lake a number of frigates and cruisers and the HMS *Harrowsmith* sat at anchor. I saw no sign of refugees, and I wondered for a moment if Thomas and I had inflated this fantasy beyond all proportion. Such a thing was impossible for me to imagine now, this small town of ours drawing to it hundreds or even thousands of people seeking safe haven. It must be that our plan was nothing but a foolish game, I remember thinking, and that I should feel ashamed for hoping to win some approval in the rescue of those less fortunate than ourselves.

When I turned to tell Sister Catherine that I should probably be on my way but that I could come back another time (though I certainly would not), I saw that she'd left the room, and in her place stood a man wearing a white lab coat over a grey suit.

"And you must be our Good Samaritan," he said.

He introduced himself as Dr. Ridley, chief administrator and medical officer at Mercy House.

"Sister Catherine tells me you're interested in lending a helping hand."

"Yes, sir."

"Fine. You're not an ophthalmologist, I take it."

"No, sir," I said.

"Optometrist?"

"No, sir," I said, confused at first. I didn't see that he was having a bit of fun.

"Splendid. Then you're an optician."

"None of those things, sir," I said.

He was not interested in finding someone to help with yardwork or general maintenance. They already had a man for that, he said. Nor was he interested in securing a helper for the nursing sisters who tended to the residents and ran the home's general operations. Nothing like that, he said. But he did have something in mind that I might possibly be suited for.

He ushered me from the room and led me along a corridor lined with more portraits of serious-looking men, long-dead lords of the great house or founders of townships and counties, I imagined, Durham and Haliburton, their names and dates inscribed on the plaques set at the bottom of each frame.

The boards underfoot creaked with each step as I followed the doctor. The house was not altogether gloomy, I began to see, or as starkly forlorn as I'd imagined a home like this must be. But I felt the stillness all around, deepened by the creaking of the floorboards.

This need of mine to prove to myself I would not be defined by my heritage was a foolish impulse I regretted more with each step. It would only get me into trouble here. *A viper is nonetheless a viper no matter where the egg is hatched.* I'd heard and read this so many times that it was hard not to believe it was true. No amount of quiet respect or number of good deeds would make any difference.

"Here we are," the doctor said, pushing open a door.

A girl was standing at the window looking out at the lake, and when she turned I saw she was the one who'd been watching us that spring and early summer all the while we'd been spying on Mercy House. She tilted her head with what looked like surprise or shock when she saw me.

"You're the younger one," she said.

1945

There were no Dutch speakers among the staff or residents at Mercy House and so the lie that they were a couple from Antwerp was not difficult to maintain. As a couple expecting a child, they were assigned one of the few private rooms—many residents were bunked six to a room, if they weren't bedridden in the hospital ward, once the grand dining hall in the east wing. Their room was hardly bigger than a closet. The weather seeped through the small window and the nearest toilet was one floor down. But a room and a bed were wild luxuries after the cold stone floor at the Parish Church.

Within days they learned the layout of the house and the rules and routines and the names of the resident physicians and the sisters who ran the hospice. Perhaps most important was the rule regarding the help at Mercy House. Silent as ghosts, these young women, whom the sisters referred to

as atonement girls, were not to be spoken to or acknowledged in any way. They would spend most of their time in
the basement, it was explained, far from the regular com-
ings and goings of the house. On occasion they would be
found upstairs, too, though, one of the sisters explained,
and in such case they would not engage the patients at all.
If for any reason one of them should speak even a single
word to any resident, the infraction was to be reported
immediately. Those people needed to learn their place, the
sister said.

Rosa held her tongue until the end of the day. "Innocent
people," she said. "And if they find out about us?"

Elser was seated on their bed, slowly taking off his shoes.
He was as disturbed as she had been to learn of the young
women who served there, condemned for nothing more
than the fact that they were German.

He continued his undressing, and then slipped into bed
and placed his hand on her abdomen, as he'd done that night
months earlier after she'd told him about the baby. She was
big now, almost eight months gone. He felt it move, but the
sense of joy that usually overcame him when this happened
did not come.

"They won't," he said. "They won't find out."

ON THE STAIRWELL UP to the second floor three days
later he stopped dead in his tracks when he suddenly felt

someone beside him. He knew it wasn't one of the other residents, whose approach was always signalled by the tapping of one of the long canes he himself used to get around the house. And the nursing sisters and doctors made it a habit to acknowledge the patients they passed in a hallway or on the stairwell. She was just inches away, this young German woman, stopped a step or two up from where he stood, frozen on her way down, he imagined, when she saw him coming up the stairs.

He heard her breathing and the creaking of the stair when she shifted her footing.

Who knew what they'd been told about the hatred these survivors held in their hearts for the Germans, for any German, and the terror she'd feel that he would report her for this encounter. He wanted to speak to her in their shared language, and tell her that he was trapped here too, just as she was, and that one day the world would come to its senses. I'm sorry, he wanted to say, but said nothing at all.

He waited another moment, acknowledged her with a slight nod, and then continued up the stairs.

ON THE FIRST WARM day of spring one of the sisters accompanied Elser and Rosa over the grounds and told them in her slow and patient English that the shipyard on the far side of the river was the source of the steam whistle blast they'd come to expect every afternoon at five. The town, just a few blocks north of where they stood, was much like any Canadian town, she said, still burdened by shortages and dependent on the Soviet aid that came up through the lifeline that was the Saint Lawrence Seaway. "The Americans have not yet begun the blockade that is expected," she said, "but we'll get by when they do, God help us."

HE BROUGHT ROSA BREAKFAST in bed now on most days as she moved towards her delivery date. At first the sisters had tolerated no exception to the mealtime schedules, but the three flights of stairs were dangerous for a pregnant blind woman, and so they allowed the privilege during these last weeks before the baby came.

In the cafeteria on the ground floor he prepared her breakfast tray of tea and toast and cereal and sometimes a cup of the Food Club tinned peaches in syrup she'd loved so much when they first arrived here. Putting this breakfast together by touch and smell was a slow and meticulous process, and delivering it up three flights of stairs, long cane in one hand, tray in the other, tested his balance and wits. Yet he made it up to their room every time without spilling a drop and set the tray with great care on the stand that still fit over her abdomen as she sat propped up in bed.

While she ate he sat with her and said what he could to convince her that they were safe in this walled sanctuary. The worst was behind them. They had a bed. They had food.

They had medical care. That was everything in a world like this. Together they would love and protect their child.

Yes, she said.

It would have a chance at a normal life.

Yes, she said. It would.

He'd lay his hand on her thigh beneath the breakfast tray and think for a moment that she was not placating him, that finally she'd chased away the fear that she'd carried in her heart since London. It was her faith in prayer, he thought. Her strength of will. When she knelt at the foot of their bed and prayed every night, it did not occur to him that she'd pray for anything other than the safe delivery of their child. Careful not to disturb her, he'd undress quietly as she performed her devotions, listening for the sound her arms made against the bedclothes. "A normal life," he said once after she'd crossed herself.

There was a pause.

"*Vipers*. That's what we are to them," she said. "Every last one of us."

SOMETIMES WHILE ROSA NAPPED in the afternoons he walked by the lake and listened to the waves washing up at the bottom of the property. It was a calming rhythm that helped take his mind away from his worries for a time. He found he was able to manage better if he did this, and if he kept moving. He needed to fill his hours with purpose.

Most days, after taking breakfast up to Rosa, he practised English with one of the sisters for an hour as she led him around the house, saying the names of things she touched his hand to—a door, a window, a table—and later he volunteered in the hospital ward in the east wing, emptying bedpans and turning the bed-bound their quarter-turns. He was limited by his blindness but determined, the sisters agreed, and able to make himself useful in a way that impressed them. When the day was fine he lifted the bedridden into wheelchairs and rolled them out to the stone terrace overlooking the lake, then brought Rosa down the three flights of stairs and walked with her over the grounds, all of this a sign of industry and hope, he thought, that she would finally take to heart.

It was different when his thoughts turned inward. He wondered if she wasn't right about everything—the baby, the future, their life here in a home for the blind in a country that condemned you for the language you spoke. He thought about the secret he held from her as he listened to the lake on those nights, the house completely still and quiet, and tried to imagine explaining to her that first, pure impulse that had pushed him on in his plan to save Germany. Wouldn't she see this now as the root cause that had led to the end of a city and her daughter's death? He could not tell her for the deep remorse and shame it raised in him, and for the fear of her condemnation.

ELSER BEGAN CONSULTATIONS IN May with the ophthalmologist named Ridley. The doctor had already spoken
to the group of likely candidates. He'd narrowed the list
down to eighteen and collected them together in the library
in the east wing. He was developing a new technique that
was not yet accepted by his peers, though it would be one
day, he said.

Elser stood at the back of the room and listened to the
man's presentation.

In the early days of his blindness he'd been able to see
faces from his past in his mind's eye. Now, months later,
these images began to fail him. His sister. His mother. They
too became ghosts, like the atonement girls who were only
ever half there, always quietly stepping away.

He understood almost nothing of what the doctor said.
Afterwards he returned to the library and found Ridley
standing by a window.

"You're DeGroote, the Dutchman," Ridley said.

"Yes."

"Soon to be a father, I hear. Congratulations."

Elser told him that he'd understood very little of his presentation, but that he'd like to see his son or daughter one
day. If only for that reason, if only for a day, he'd do whatever
necessary. It was a simple and moving plea. For the next two
hours Ridley attempted to explain the procedure, stopping
often to ask if he was being understood. He backtracked,

explained again, repeated himself—all this in a patient and forgiving voice.

Ridley had discovered something crucial during the terrible months he'd treated fighter pilots from the 601 Squadron wounded during the Battle of Britain. After acrylic plastics started being used in the Spitfire canopy, he went on—yes, do you understand *canopy*?—he'd noticed less inflammation in the damaged eye. "Plastic instead of glass, you understand? That's what made the difference." The damage was there, of course, when the shards from the canopy entered the eye, but the plastic caused no inflammation. Just tearing of the cornea. It was the unique qualities found in the acrylic plastics that inspired his research and tests now, he said. He was developing a new intraocular lens made of plastic similar to the plastic used in the Spitfire canopy.

"Do you understand?"

Elser was not at all confident he'd grasped the mechanics of the procedure, but he said that he was ready to do what was required.

THE MAJORITY OF THE patients at Mercy House had suffered the permanent retinal damage of flash blindness. They would never see again. "But cataracts are a completely different story," Ridley said at their second consultation. "A physical barrier, nothing more. We've removed these for centuries, with varying degrees of success. A disc of protein obstructs vision, as it has in your case, and your wife's case. The new idea is this: we replace the cataract with the artificial lens. Acrylic, you understand, is the difference. A plastic lens, not glass. Science makes its greatest advances in wartime. One of the great ironies of our times."

They were seated across from each other in the wood-and-plaster cottage that Ridley used as his consultation and operating rooms. He got up and came around from his side of the desk, took hold of Elser's right hand, and placed it on a globe-sized model of the human eye.

"The mystery of sight at your fingertips," he said.

He told him the names of these parts of the eye as he led Elser's fingers over the puzzle—the cornea, the aqueous humour, the iris, the lens.

He would make the incision here through which he'd remove the cataract, then irrigate the remaining lens fragments, washing them out from under the aqueous humour, here, he said, directing Elser's fingers, and implant the new lens and seal the incision with stitching. Simple and miraculous, he said.

"Two hours per eye, perhaps. And after a forty-eight-hour recovery period the bandages will come off and then you will see your newborn."

IN EARLY JULY, FIVE days before he was to undergo his surgery, Rosa leaned forward in mid-sentence and began to breathe in shortened, strained breaths. She placed her weight against the bureau, causing it to shift and bump against the wall. An anguished sound emerged from deep in her throat.

Elser helped her into their bed, covered her with a blanket, and went to tell the sisters that the baby was on its way.

After he returned, he sat at Rosa's bedside while Sister Evelyn assessed the situation. She told him they'd call if they needed him, but he was to leave the room now, he would only get in the way here. He held Rosa's hand and told her he'd be close by, downstairs, just a few rooms away.

On the main floor he paced nervously until well past midnight. He was alone. There was nothing to do. He stood at a window, waiting helplessly, listening to the lake at the bottom of the property. The sound was smooth and rhythmical, like calm, steady breathing.

His wife's muted cries punctuated the silence of the sleeping house soon after that. They sent waves of fear through his heart. Undisturbed, the other residents of the house slept on. He went back upstairs after the cries stopped but the nurses shooed him away a second time.

BEFORE DAWN SISTER EVELYN found him slumped in a chair by the fireplace, half asleep. She told him the hot water tank was not refilling fast enough. Rosa had been in the bath for hours. He was to fetch some hot water up from the scullery, and he was to go at once.

It was a small errand he took pleasure in, finally able to do something useful. He knew the house well enough, its vast rooms and narrow corridors.

He found the door to the pantry off the kitchen and tapped his cane down the flight of stairs. It was a place he'd never been before, reserved as it was for the atonement girls who served there. The steps were tricky going for a blind man, steeper than the others in the house, he found. With great care he felt his way to the bottom of the staircase, then stood a moment, listening.

A woman's voice called out. "Yes? Who is it?" she said.

She would not be used to seeing anyone this early in the day, he knew, let alone a resident. He didn't approach.

"Sister Evelyn sent me. For hot water. My wife—"

He knew she was frightened and stopped speaking mid-sentence. She was studying his face, he imagined, wondering about the dangers of him coming down here and about the punishment she'd receive for having anything at all to do with him. He repeated that it was Sister Evelyn who'd sent him, that permission had been granted, and then he heard her footsteps on the stone floor and a moment later the sound of a cauldron being filled with water and lifted and set on the cast-iron stovetop.

He came forward a few steps and waited at the door and listened as she moved about the scullery. He wanted to tell her that she needn't be afraid of him and that she could tell him what she knew about the world out there. Was it as bad here for people like us as they said? He wanted to ask a hundred questions about the town and the country he'd been brought to, and about her, this silent German girl who'd been forbidden to speak her language, but he could not be sure she wouldn't betray him for the prize of discovering his secret.

She lifted the cauldron off the stovetop and placed it on the floor at his feet, as he had suspected she would, its swing handle positioned upwards. She would do what she could to avoid having their hands touch, even in passing the pot from one to another, so afraid of the cancers that seemed to touch most of them here.

He took it without a word and carried the boiling water upstairs to where a nursing sister met him in the hallway outside their room. She took the cauldron and said they would find him when there was news.

He tapped his way back down to the main floor and settled in the chair he'd been roused from half an hour earlier. He heard movement upstairs, creaking floors and bedroom doors opening and closing.

The house was waking up.

Just after seven, Sisters Cecilia and Harriette entered the parlour and he stood and asked if they wouldn't go see for him if there was any news. Sister Harriette left him in the company of Sister Cecilia, who sat with him in silence until two ladies, Mrs. Larson and Mrs. Starmer, came downstairs and suggested he join them for breakfast in the dining hall.

"Best stay busy at a time like this," one of them said.

"A watched pot never boils," the other said.

He did not know the idiom, of course, which they began to explain to him as they carried him on into their morning.

An hour later Sister Caroline came with the news. The mother was fine.

"Your wife is a strong woman," she said, taking his arm and leading him from the dining hall to a room on the second floor.

"Your wife is resting upstairs," the sister said. "This is your daughter."

She placed the newborn in his arms, and when his stiffness grew apparent she positioned his hands for him and he thanked her.

The sister waited a moment, already heartbroken.

"To this place of damnation good things rarely come," she said.

He heard the motion of her hand performing the four movements in the sign of the cross.

"What is it?" he said.

"It's not for us to understand God's will, but we must bear it nonetheless."

She took one of his hands out from under the child, slowly, giving him time to adjust his hold, and placed his fingers on the deformity.

STILL SHAKEN, HE JOINED Rosa in their room on the third floor and sat at her bedside and tried to think of something to say. They sat in silence for a time. It was as if neither of them would ever speak again or feel anything other than the searing grief that cut them now.

Their daughter was healthy otherwise, he wanted to say, there was that at least. They could make do, teach her to live a normal life. It was an absurd thought. He knew nothing about normal life anymore. It was too far behind him in a remote and vanishing world. He held her as she wept and wondered why God had chosen to punish her and the child and not him and only him for the horror he'd caused.

There was nothing to say, there could be no consolation. The embrace was silent, each lost in their thoughts, until one of the sisters brought the baby in for a feeding.

The helpless creature was crying when the sister gave her to Rosa, propped up now in the bed, but the crying fell silent when she began to nurse and the suckling and small panting between gulps brought Elser's heart to the top of his throat. After the baby was finished he held her in his arms, silently pacing the room, while Rosa tried to rest.

Next to the bed that night, he listened to his wife and daughter sleep. He drifted off once and awoke to the sound of the contented suckling that again helped him to believe that the sense of defeat that had consumed them might eventually lift. In it he heard an appetite for life, a hunger that ignored hesitation or doubt, the pure instinct to travel forward. What he felt was something that approached happiness and the simple pleasure of fatherhood. It surprised him. He wanted to share this tenderness with his wife. He wanted to reach through the darkness to touch her and to communicate the startling thought that here in the ruins of their life they'd found the simple blessed possibility that would offer them courage and joy and make disappear for them all the dangers that awaited.

SHE HEARD HIS BREATHING deepen into the slow rhythm of sleep and whispered his name three times to be sure. She felt under her pillow for the glass ampule she'd taken from the medical bag that had been left untended that day and cracked it open with her teeth.

He did not wake up. The baby didn't stir.

She felt the cold begin to crawl through her veins almost immediately after taking the liquid on her tongue. She'd bargained with God, negotiated with men, and pleaded with doctors. Nothing had helped. Neither God nor man had listened, and so she would provide her own answer. Courage did not fail her this time. She asked her daughter's forgiveness as she lay waiting. One day she'd understand, perhaps even wonder how her mother had held on for so long in such a world. With her last breath the broken ampule rolled from her hand.

THE CAUSE OF DEATH would not be spoken of, the sisters decided, and so when Sister Evelyn brought Lina Teufel up to the screened-in verandah on the second floor that morning, she mentioned only that the man's wife had died in the night.

Lina knew only that motherhood meant a price was to

be paid, sometimes as high as the one exacted of the poor woman whose child she was handed that day. Her own suffering had been nowhere as severe as this child's mother's, she knew. The birth of her son Thomas had been uneventful, agonizing beyond measure, but natural after all. It was a grim understanding for Lina when she knew at last that having her son would not make her life better, or bring fulfillment, or cause her to love her husband more. The child was work. Endless work. And this while the duties at Mercy House asked more and more of her. The old German woman who came down from the camp every morning to look after Thomas helped some, but she was a hardened Berliner who chose not to disguise her suspicion of this woman who lived in town and ate decent food for the simple reason that she'd married a half-German.

The nursing had always been difficult, at times agonizing, but it was the silent killer Lina feared when she held the woman's child at her breast that first morning, deformed as it was, and when the baby was finished, she buttoned her uniform back up to the neck and passed it to Sister Evelyn. She got up and prepared to leave. She was trembling and at the point of tears.

"That will be all," the sister said.

"Yes, ma'am," Lina said, as she'd been taught.

Elser recognized her voice from the scullery two nights ago and heard the door open and her footsteps moving down the hallway, stepping quickly, and then running.

1960

Muriel was wearing a formless grey jumper and dark stockings the day Dr. Ridley introduced us at Mercy House. He'd walked me along that creaking hallway to a room filled with books, and there I saw a tall girl of about my brother's age standing at the window. She turned and saw me and said that thing about me being the younger one, which seemed to register an attitude somewhere between disappointment and resignation, and I shrugged with embarrassment.

She was taller than me by half a head, her eyes searching and intelligent, and what I felt more than the disappointing fact that I'd let her down as the younger of two brothers was the confusing thrill that I'd discovered someone of roughly my own age living here, who, oddly, was not blind.

"I'll be thirteen this summer, anyway," I said, eager just then to hurry along my birthday. She didn't seem friendly in the least, or at all impressed that I was here. She shrugged her shoulders and said she'd turned fifteen just a few weeks ago.

"Muriel's never met anyone her own age before—much less a boy," Dr. Ridley said.

She'd lived in the hospice her whole life, I learned later, but at this point, still knowing next to nothing about her, I decided we were two peas in a pod. If anything, she was even more of an outcast than I was. You only had to look at that defiant, sullen face to know that she felt the same way about people as I did—that quick as a whip they'd round on you for an easy laugh in the schoolyard, find some difference to exploit as best they could, or push your face in the mud for the sin of sticking up for yourself.

"So, it would seem you're a novelty here, son," Dr. Ridley said. "Muriel might just have to pinch you to believe you're real."

"I've seen them down there a million times. Throwing stones and branches and spying on us," she told the doctor.

"I'd rue the day a boy loses his curiosity to know the world," Dr. Ridley said.

I was embarrassed to be caught out so quickly, to understand that she knew who I was and what my brother and I were always up to when we peered over the stone wall, watching the house. As we stood staring at each other for ten long seconds of silence before Sister Catherine returned to ask for Dr. Ridley's assistance, I recognized in her something that I'd never seen in anyone else before. She was even more desperate and helpless than I was, it seemed, and I believed I'd finally found someone who might become a friend.

"I wonder about *those* two sometimes," Muriel said, mooning her eyes with great delight once the doctor and the sister were gone. The absence of adults, something she hardly knew, seemed exciting to her. And it was as if in an instant she'd deemed me worthy of her confidence, though I didn't fully grasp why, or what she was implying. What *did* she wonder about them? I thought.

"I watch people around here," she said. "There's always something going on that they want to hide from you."

Her irreverence baffled and alarmed me. It was also thrilling. I'd never heard anyone talk like that, let alone a boy or a girl, and the private lives of adults had always struck me as the last thing on earth you wanted to think about as a kid.

"I see how you always do what your brother tells you. I see that in the way you nod your head when he speaks to you. You follow him around like a puppy."

The idea that we were both lonely kids destined to become friends began to feel remote now. Deflated, I wondered if she wasn't just like any other kid looking for a way to make me feel like an idiot. I wondered if it wasn't inherent in people, this bullying impulse. It was true what she'd said about me being a follower, but I didn't need reminding of the fact.

"It was my idea to come here. He doesn't know where I am," I said.

She seemed to think about that for a moment, and then she said, "Do you know what Braille is? Practically everyone here knows it. We have books in Braille, but mostly we have regular books. A whole library full. They like it when I read to them. I'm probably the best-read kid of all time."

Her favourite book, she said—and for reasons that should have become clear to me as she retold the story—was *The Count of Monte Cristo*.

We stayed up there talking about the stories we liked. I told her about my comic book collection and the hero named Doctor Atom and his laser-beam eyes. She thought that was great, the way he reduced the German occupiers in London to one smoking heap of ash after another. She'd never seen a comic book before. I told her with no confidence at all that I'd be happy to bring one the next time I visited, and she nodded and said she'd like that.

My mother had never mentioned anyone having a baby at Mercy House in her day—other than herself, of course, and the other atonement girl who'd told her how to protect her child against radiation sickness—but it was a big house and, according to her stories, she spent almost all of her time there in the basement.

As Muriel showed me around the house that day, I wanted to ask her about her parents, but I didn't want to upset her. I imagined they were both in that small graveyard by the chapel that she never took me to. I followed her down the stairs to the main floor and past a door that led, according to Muriel, to the scullery and pantry—where *those ladies* had worked, she said. No one went down there anymore, not since the last of the atonement girls had left, back when she was still little. I couldn't help but imagine my mother down there, of course. It was a grim-looking door, if a simple wooden door with a brass knob and hinges can look grim, but it was through that portal my mother had disappeared every day for five years, and to no good end, and I was relieved when Muriel told me to hurry along, there was more to see.

We walked through a maze of rooms, each sparsely furnished and empty of people but for the second-to-last room, in which four residents sat playing dominoes. None of them seemed to notice when we walked past them. One of them, a man seated in a wheelchair, traced his fingers over the cross that was the patchwork of dominoes set out on the green card table before placing his tile, then raised his hand and said something in a language I'd never heard before. It was just something that Mr. Mulligan did, Muriel said, identifying the man by his name. Before the war he'd taught Latin at Trinity College Dublin, she said.

We ended up in the library on the far side of the house that day. It was a big, beautiful room with high ceilings and heavy chairs and a thick red rug and green lamps set on the end tables.

"You'll like this place if you like books," she said. "We don't have any of those comics you're talking about. These were all here when the sisters came. You can borrow *The Count of Monte Cristo* if you like."

She began scanning the shelves for the title, her eyes travelling along the colourful spines. She moved to the next shelf, then the next, and finally declared that one of the staff must be reading it now.

"How about this one instead?" she said, turning back to me.

She handed it over, thumb forward on its cover, fingers obscured underneath. It was a science fiction novel called *The Butterfly Cage* by someone named Kilgore Trout that told of a future society that recreated its ancestors with a machine of such terrific power that the people in those recreations didn't know they weren't real. She loved that part, Muriel said, but the twist was even better. The simulations were turned into penal colonies that held generations of those who were made to pay for the sins of their forefathers.

"And why would they do that?" I said. It seemed an unlikely scenario to me. What I knew of science fiction was limited to *Lost in Space* and *The Twilight Zone*, programs my father and Thomas did their best to watch most Sunday evenings.

"Because the sins are so terrible that the punishment can never end," Muriel said. "The girl in the story begins to understand why she's really there. She's the only one who knows, you see. She figures it out when she starts noticing things. Weird repetitions, like déjà vu. You know that feeling? And things disappear and reappear again without explanation. One time she sees her own face in a cloud while she's walking to school."

"Does she get out?" I said.

"I'm not going to ruin it for you—you'll just have to read it."

She turned and scanned the shelves with the air of a connoisseur engaged in the serious business of choosing only the best of what is on offer. It took her a moment, this serious deliberation, then she said, "Presto. How about this one? In this one the good guys win. The Americans get in the war and drop the bomb on the *Japanese* and the Germans end up with only half a country. Which you'd think is a stretch. But they make it sound real."

I didn't want to read a story about the war, no matter how badly the Germans took it in the teeth. I told her I'd give the first one a try, and when I took *The Butterfly Cage* from her I saw what she'd been hiding from me this whole time.

I recoiled, almost dropping the book.

She brought her hands into her armpits and glowered at me. "You know it's not polite to stare," she said.

"I'm sorry," I muttered.

We stood there in a silence filled with the strange formality that suddenly re-established itself over us, and then she brought her hands up close to my face and said, "So what does that make me—a monster?"

There were only two fingers and a thumb on each hand, clawed and frightening to look at, like twisted tree roots.

"That's why you don't go to school," I said.

"No ghouls at school, right? Isn't that what everyone would say?"

It was exactly what everyone would say. She'd be teased and taunted in a way that'd make what they did to me feel like a clumsy pat on the head. "They're all idiots anyway," I said.

She put her hands in the pockets of her jumper and rolled her shoulders. "You'd better go."

I didn't know if this was her attempt to release me from the shame and embarrassment that had risen between us or if she'd simply given up on me. I'd been her first test and had crashed out miserably. I wanted to tell her that I was sorry for the reaction I'd shown, but the apology I struggled with as I stood there became blurred with my own discomfort. It was only seconds that passed, I'm sure, and before I knew it she was leading me from the library and down the panelled hallway in the direction we'd come. We were more alike than she could ever know. That's what I wanted to tell her, but I was not strong enough.

I was surprised that she walked me all the way to my bike. I held the copy of *The Butterfly Cage* out to her. I'd almost forgotten it was still in my hand.

She shook her head. "Fair trade for some of those comic books you were talking about," she said, and turned and started down the lane.

AT HOME, I SAT on the front steps until supper that evening after hiding the novel under my pillow and wondered if I shouldn't tell Thomas what I'd discovered. The shipyard steam whistle sounded from across the river at five, and twenty minutes later my father came cutting across the field opposite the house, his hard hat pushed back on his forehead. He walked with a full, leisurely stride that looked strong and determined and made me proud that he was my father. He waved to me and came over the lawn and up the stairs and sat down beside me. He took the hard hat off his head and placed it on mine and tapped it twice, the way he used to when I was younger. The two taps indicated that I was in charge now. I liked it when he did that. It was our little game, one he was willing to play with a kid who wasn't in charge of anything at all. He asked me what I'd gotten up to today, but I wasn't able to say anything about Muriel, though I wanted to. Now I wasn't sure I hadn't done something terribly wrong in visiting the house. My going there had nothing to do with generosity or sacrifice. I'd only wanted to make myself feel better, and my father would have seen right through me.

We played chess in the backyard that evening. Here I had another chance to tell him what I'd been up to, but I kept this guilty secret to myself. I usually liked playing chess with my father. I enjoyed the game itself, I suppose. But more than this, I liked having my father all to myself when we played. I liked how sometimes we didn't talk for what seemed like hours but hovered there in this wordless exchange, both of us focused and eager to see what would happen next. He usually won. I got lucky once in a while. I don't recall him ever saying that he enjoyed spending time with just me, though—with Thomas off doing whatever he did while we played—but I wanted to believe that it was these quiet moments together as much as the game itself that accounted for this evening ritual of ours.

Sometimes a bead of resin dripped from one of the big spruce trees that darkened the south side of the house. If it fell on one of his pieces—a rook or a pawn or whatever— he'd wipe it clean and return it to the board but intentionally misplace it on a square that offered a more direct attack on my king. I never noticed this sleight of hand. After I made my next move, he'd put his hand on mine and ask if the board looked right to me. I'd study it with great focus, and then he'd remind me that I had to keep my eyes open, there were always cheats out there looking to take advantage, and he'd return the man to its proper place, which then looked right to me, and we'd continue playing.

I wasn't able to concentrate that evening. After he won three quick games we shook hands as we always did and packed up the set.

I was still trying to make sense of that afternoon and the strange girl I'd met. That book of hers was waiting for me upstairs. I wondered if it had something to tell me about her that she couldn't tell me herself. I carried the chessboard inside and left it on the coffee table on my way upstairs. The book wasn't under my pillow where I'd put it when I got home. I wondered if Thomas had found it, but I could think of no reason he'd go snooping around under my pillow. I got down on my hands and knees and looked under both our beds. I checked our closet and desk drawers and the pile of socks and underwear and T-shirts in our dresser. The model airplanes strung from the ceiling flew on, searching for a kill. The book was gone.

I WENT BACK TO Mercy House the following day, and at no time then or on any of my subsequent visits in the weeks to come did Muriel ask about the book I'd lost or the comics I'd told her about.

It was mid-July now and the arrival of refugees from across the lake continued in a steady drip, this according to the news reports, but the exodus we'd heard was on its way was too small to help move along the plan my brother and I had dreamed up. The memory of that salute rolled around in my head constantly, but not only for the fact that it could get us thrown out of our own home. The thought that I couldn't be sure who he was anymore terrified me. Days went by when I hardly saw him at all between breakfast and suppertime. All of a sudden it seemed a line had been drawn between us.

In the morning I usually rode to the hospice and watched the house until Muriel appeared and waved from the window. She didn't come down to meet me every time, though. Far from it. And sometimes she didn't wave at all. I wondered if I'd done something wrong on some previous visit, offended her in some way. By then she'd met me at the gate four or five times, and each time I had done my best not to look at her hands or to say anything about school or being normal or the circumstances that had brought her there in the first place. I worried about my own hands, in fact—outwardly they were healed well enough now, but I still struggled with the idea that my blood had been contaminated. Sometimes I felt a tingling in my fingertips at night as I lay in bed trying to fall asleep. I grew convinced this had something to do with the smoke the Russian inspector had blown over my cuts. During the day it didn't worry me so much, but at night my mind seemed to travel a million miles an hour, and always in some doomsday direction. And so as often as possible I rode down there come morning and watched for her at the window, eager for the friendship and the distraction that would help get me out of my own head.

One day she ventured out, but she didn't see me. She walked over the gravel drive and turned right, in the direction of the chapel and the small cemetery, and I wondered if she was going to visit her parents' graves there. I backed away from the gate, sorry that I'd caught her in this private moment. It was impossible not to feel foolish as I stood there on the mornings she ignored me. There were days I waited for an hour or more before I gave up. I never went right home after that. My mother would have asked what was wrong. Had I met some boys who were bothering me? Was I thinking about next year, school and bullies? She was good at noticing my moods, maybe because she felt things as deeply as I did. She worried about everything. I wanted to spare her that. I'd stay out as long as I could, as if I was happily distracted, just being a kid, but mostly I just rode around the neighbourhood, or ended up standing on the pier looking for my father in the forest of tower cranes that grew on the other side of the river.

There was a lighthouse at the end of the pier where you'd always see one or two fishermen going for pike and bass on the harbour side, or trying for the big carp that travelled a bit farther out in the lake in schools so numerous and close to the surface that you would could see their wake from a hundred yards off. There were always a dozen or more cargo ships at anchor just off shore. These were impressive enough, each as big as our whole town it seemed from where I stood, but more thrilling than these were the Tiger-class battle cruisers that patrolled our side of the lake. There were six of them out there to match the half dozen American cruisers on the other side, this determined by the treaty that dictated the number and class of naval vessels permitted on the four Great Lakes we shared with the United States. Sometimes one of our cruisers came in close enough to the harbour that you could see its twin gun mounts, and once I saw the turrets begin to turn, as if tracking an invisible target. Fearful that a new war was about to begin, I pressed my hands over my ears. But the big cannons stayed silent that day and I heard only the muted laughter of the fishermen at the end of the pier, which shamed me into knowing I could never be as indifferent or as brave as them.

ONE MORNING IN EARLY August I waited for Muriel by the stone wall longer than usual. It might have been a whole week of being ignored since she'd last come down to see me, but even a friend as unpredictable as this would be more than I'd ever had before. She came across the lawn from behind the house and opened the gate and told me she had something important to show me. She didn't say what but I didn't need much convincing. I ditched my bike and followed her, gravel crunching underfoot, wondering what the big secret was.

The idea that Mercy House might be a place she'd want to get away from had occurred to me more than once, of course, and I considered that, like the hero of the *Monte Cristo* story, she might be thinking about getting out of there for good. The thought that she was going to ask me for help made me feel good, though just exactly what I'd be able to do for her was beyond me.

I noticed that her grey socks were pulled high to the knee, leaving a narrow band of pink skin above, which I watched as I caught up with her. The hem of her jumper was wet— from a garden hose, from the lake, I didn't know—but it was the secret of her body that took my imagination at that moment, and the feeling hit with a force that surprised me.

The only thing I knew about girls then was that one might lift or bury my spirits with the turn of an eye. I wondered if the secret she'd mentioned had something to do with sex— not actual sex, of course, but something that skirted the subject. I'd heard the word *petting* before and other sorts of rough talk in the schoolyard, but these things, beyond their general meanings, signified little to me. I imagined I was on the edge of some groundbreaking discovery, and I felt my heart race and my stomach turn in knots.

"But let's go to the house first," she said. "We'll need to bring something to eat."

I felt relieved and let down at the same time, and then a wave of nerves hit me again, and finally I was convinced that I had no idea what she wanted of me.

Since the day Sister Catherine had introduced me to Dr. Ridley and Muriel, more than four weeks earlier, I'd entered the house only once, and just briefly, to use the washroom.

The dining hall was in a large room fitted out with cafeteria and buffet tables set with salvers of hot and cold food, coffee and juice dispensers, and plates, teacups, glassware, and cutlery. The sister seated at a table near the door smiled at us and returned to the open Bible in front of her. Muriel led me to the buffet table and stacked her plate with breakfast buns and an apple. We sat and ate our buns as the room slowly filled with the old, blind residents. They tapped and swung their canes before them as they spread throughout the room to the tables and chairs they'd occupied, I imagined, since the day of their arrival years earlier, or moved directly to the buffet tables against the wall opposite where we sat.

The dining hall was not as loud as the lunchroom I knew at school, of course, but there was about it a hum of voices and a scraping of chairs against hardwood floors. As we ate Muriel spoke in a near-whisper about the people at various tables. She spoke of her housemates as a collector speaks of some rare assortment of hidden treasures, all so very odd and uniquely hers. The fact that she'd grown up here meant she knew everything about it, and I knew nothing at all. She was here to show off her collection of rarities. Each of them had a story which she shared a bit of with me. Miss Hollingshead, over there, had been a math teacher before the war. Mr. McNally, the man holding his fork with his left hand, a cobbler. Mr. Conacher, beside the woman with the witchy nose, had been a mining engineer who'd returned to London from an expedition in Northern Ontario only days before the bomb was dropped.

Most of them looked impossibly old to me, beyond ancient, with their skin loose and their bones buckling them to a near-simian crouch, though later I learned that the oldest person there wasn't yet sixty. The older people had already died. Despite their relative youth, they moved with difficulty, hunched and drawn. Their hands shook with tremors as they ate. The Latin scholar, Mr. Mulligan, whom I'd seen playing dominoes on my first visit, was confined to a wheelchair, as were almost half of the people there. Those who could still walk made their way with the aid of a cane Muriel called a Hoover stick, a number of which I'd seen collected in the ceramic vase at the bottom of the main stairs on the day of my first visit.

Within the hour I'd learn the real reason she'd brought me there. But as she took me around the dining hall, introducing me as if we were old friends, I wondered if this wasn't what she'd intended to show me. The surprising camaraderie, the casualness of it all. The mood wasn't at all what I'd expected. These people were sick and some looked terribly old, but none demonstrated the sort of anger or self-pity I'd prepared myself for. I was simply an innocent visitor invited in by Sister Catherine and approved by Dr. Ridley to be a friend to the unfortunate girl they'd known since her birth. I wasn't expecting them to show anger or to be suspicious of me. None of them had any idea that I was the son of one of the German girls who'd worked there years ago. The reception they gave me would have been different if they had, I'm sure of it. Under the terms of service there she'd been a nonentity, and as I walked through the dining hall with Muriel that morning it hit me as if for the first time that this place had been as much a prison to my mother as it was to these survivors of London.

"You've brought a friend along!" one of the ladies, a certain Mrs. Hastings, said. "I've heard from the sisters."

Muriel turned to me and rolled her eyes as if to say, *Isn't this a hoot?*

"His name is Graham," she said, using the name I'd provided Sister Catherine the day I walked up the laneway for the first time.

It was hard to imagine this woman as a sighted person, which she'd presumably been before the flash of the bomb blinded her, and harder yet to imagine why Muriel had done her best to make fun of her.

"Well, dear boy," the woman said, "we shouldn't keep you two a moment longer. Run along with your friend now and enjoy the day."

"He's left the room already, quick as a jackrabbit!" Muriel said, rolling her eyes again. She raised a finger to her lips to silence me.

I was stricken with shame for my part in the conspiracy. But I didn't say anything. I held still, afraid she might discover Muriel's lie, pinned there by this unpleasant game.

"Well, dear," she said, "boys can be timid creatures, after all. Especially at that age. Perhaps we've overwhelmed him with this display of our misfortune."

Muriel may have liked these people, even loved them, but this was how she entertained herself in a world that was otherwise mirthless and static. That was the only explanation that occurred to me as we silently exited the dining hall; I tried to remember that I was an outsider and knew nothing of these people and the rules of the house.

We found a spot by a big maple and shared another bun that Muriel had taken from the buffet table. I was pleased she'd done so. I was still hungry. It was probably past nine o'clock and I'd had my own breakfast early. She was more relaxed than when she'd first met me at the gate an hour or so earlier, and I wondered about my own nervous thoughts that had possessed me. Thinking this made me feel even more ashamed, and I was relieved at least to have witnessed something shameful Muriel had done too. We were in the same boat, and now we could start our morning over again fresh.

She was testing me—I know this now—and I'd passed the test, though to what end I still had no idea. I'd not betrayed her in the game she'd played on her housemate. I could be trusted. Still clueless, I wanted to ask why she'd done such a spiteful and humiliating thing to poor Mrs. Hastings. It was a fun thing to do, I imagined she'd tell me, and just because everyone was blind here didn't mean you couldn't have a sense of humour. That was what I suspected was behind the deceit. But I was wrong. It was a test for what was to come. Without knowing it, I'd proven myself trustworthy, and to my own shame I'd passed her shabby examination.

The day began to feel different to me as we sat there, talking and eating. My serious nature did not allow me to find anything funny about what she'd done. I'd not suffered a scintilla compared to what she'd suffered, yet she was able to find irreverence and humour here. This was nearly as great a puzzle to me as the looming question of sex was in these early days of my adolescence. I felt the beginnings of something I would never properly understand, which was the uneven nature of suffering in the face of tragedy. We were both liars, granted, but my lies found their origin in the shame that ruled me. Hers were for sport, it seemed. She'd deceived the lady in some attempt to poke fun, to find strength perhaps in the pleasure of controlling the people around her. I lied about my identity every day I came to be with Muriel. In my head I'd created a sympathetic story for her that might accommodate a girl who'd grown up in a place like this. But all I had on offer was sympathy. I couldn't fit that girl into what I knew of Muriel now. She didn't seem as torqued out of proportion as those hands of hers suggested she might be.

When she finished the last of the bun we'd torn in half, she tilted her head back and closed her eyes, as if appreciating the powerful energies around her. She waited like that for a minute or two, eyes still closed, as I inched my way through these confusing thoughts. I recognized my need now. I wanted her to tell me how sad she was, what a terrible fate it was to be stuck here, and that she didn't like making fun of the people she'd known her whole life, that being around sick people made her want to cry all the time, and now she was ashamed of herself. There could be no other reality running through her mind, I decided. I was preparing to love her then. I'd commit to her every last ounce of sympathy available to me because I didn't understand love, or that those you profess to love need more than I was able to give, hobbled as I was by my incomplete and selfish sympathy. It was all the love I could find, though, what I felt for her at that moment, and I wanted to give it to her, and for her to keep it and to use it to help her understand who I was.

She reached into a small side pocket of her jumper and produced a cigarette and matches, and struck a match against the tree bark. The flame jumped to life. She brought the flame to the cigarette she held at the side of her mouth.

"I'll bet you've never smoked, right?"

I told her no, I hadn't.

"Everybody here smokes. I have lots of these. I get them from the ladies. The men usually carry theirs everywhere. In their shirt pockets and all that. The ladies leave them in their rooms. Easy pickings. I help myself."

I'd never stolen anything from anyone as far as I could remember. I didn't know what to make of the fact that she'd told me this, like it was nothing at all, even though it was just a handful of dumb cigarettes. I watched her take a few puffs, practising in my head how I'd do it. I knew she'd expect me to try one. Even with hands as disfigured as hers she knew how to hold a cigarette better than I could. I couldn't think of a single thing I'd do better than her—other than simply being a kid with normal hands. She closed her eyes when she held it to her mouth, then sent luxurious puffs over her head. I liked how the ember lit up when she drew on the cigarette, and how she seemed to chew and then to swallow the smoke and finally expel it when she was good and ready, with no rush at all, in rings that quivered for a moment before they broke apart. When she offered to teach me she extended the cigarette in a conspiratorial fashion, looking this way and that. I still wasn't used to her hands. I made sure not to touch her when she passed me the cigarette. I took a puff, coughed, and gave it back to her.

She didn't seem to care one way or the other that I didn't know how to smoke. She was two years older than me. I wondered if she just didn't expect much from a kid my age.

She blew another cloud of smoke between us, and went on to say that dozens of people had died there since she was born. "That's why I'm like this," she said, wiggling the cigarette between her fingers. "I guess you figured that out."

I didn't tell her that my brother and I called it Radiation Row down here, but I can't imagine that would have surprised her.

"There's probably ghosts, too. With all the people who've died here. I've never seen any. But it makes sense. If there're ghosts anywhere in the world they'd be here."

She took one last puff and flicked the cigarette away, then stretched out an arm and laid her hand, palm up, on my knee. I didn't know what she was doing. She took my hand in hers and rested one of my fingers against her skin, on her arm, and closed her eyes. "You trace your way up and down, and I'll stop you when you come to the inner elbow."

I was glad I had Muriel to myself. Thomas was always much better at everything we did together, and I knew he would've taken over our time together. But I was terrified now. The back of her palm was still lying in my lap. I didn't know what to do. I pointed somewhere on her forearm.

"No, no—touch me. Like this," she said. She took my wrist, just as the Russian inspector had, and told me to shut my eyes. "You tell me when."

Of course I was afraid to touch her. But suddenly it wasn't her hands I was afraid of. It was the age-old reason: she was a girl and I was a boy, and I didn't know what she wanted with me.

I'd played this game before. It was a fun way to see how eager your arm was to trick you into believing the other person's finger had found the inner crease of your elbow. I was always fooled in the end, tricked every time. So when her finger touched my arm I jumped a bit, wanting to tell her that she was already there. But I knew enough to wait. An intense sensation was gathering there. It was different from when my brother did this. Now it was a conspicuous feeling. It was pleasurable. I liked it. I closed my eyes. I'd not thought of her like this until now, as a girl I'd maybe like to kiss, and who might like to kiss me, and then, just as suddenly, she told me she was ready to show me that surprise she'd mentioned at the gate.

I was too afraid not to follow her. By now I was convinced this surprise had something to do with me, or us, and I was eager and terrified in equal measure to find out what it was. I followed her to the east side of the house and in through a mudroom door that led to the corridor she'd taken me down that day she showed me the library. I knew where she was taking me now, but I had no idea what she had in mind for us in the basement scullery where my mother had spent her days here. It was abandoned now, she'd said, unused and forgotten.

The way was lit by a naked bulb that hung from a wire at the bottom of the stairs. I followed her, hand gripping the wooden rail. The air smelled of wet stone and dirt and mildew. My heart was racing. When we got to the bottom of the stairs I saw another light coming from a room at the end of a short passageway. I felt relief at seeing this, thinking that the place was not as abandoned as I'd thought. Perhaps she came down here often and it was not so forlorn as I'd felt it to be. The walls were of the same stone as the walls that bordered the estate itself, taken from nearby fields, I imagined, before people came and put houses there, and they were lined with warped wooden shelving cluttered with cardboard boxes and pots and dusty glassware. The floor was packed dirt.

"This way, just in here," Muriel said.

We entered what once had been the scullery but now seemed a catch-all for everything the house had decided to discard. It was littered with stacks of newspapers and piles of what looked like old clothing and pillows and shoes heaped against the far wall. A kerosene lamp burned at a low flame on a table in the centre of the room. The thought that my mother had spent so many days in this dreary place was a depressing one.

"No one even comes down here. It's all mine," Muriel said.

When I noticed the ratty old mattress on the floor in the

corner I wondered if that was where I was supposed to sit her down and kiss her. By now I felt convinced that this was why she'd brought me here. I feared that I was supposed to show her that I was more than the boy I appeared to be, that I had some experience in these things.

And then, taking the apple from the dining hall out of her pocket and shining it against her jumper, she told me she had something to show me. She got down on one knee and rolled it towards the heap of clothing.

The apple bumped and bounced over the dirt floor and came to rest at the bottom of the pile. The clothing had been worn by patients who'd died since coming to Mercy House, I decided. The pile probably glowed in the dark when that kerosene lamp wasn't lit. That's why it was burning now, I thought. To hide the glow so I wouldn't turn and run.

I didn't know what she wanted from me. The kiss I'd imagined seemed impossible now, and I wondered if she wanted to make me as sick as her by bringing me here and exposing me to all that radiation-soaked clothing. At the very least she was making fun of me, the way she'd made a fool of that poor old lady in the dining hall, telling her I'd left when I was standing right there in front of her.

I looked across the dim room to the apple, about to tell her I was leaving. It was sitting there at the edge of the pile of clothing. And then the pile shifted slightly and a small hand emerged, took hold of the fruit, and disappeared again.

SHE WAS A SIX-YEAR-OLD Jewish kid from Ilium, New York, alone now but for me and Muriel, who'd brought her down here to wait while she figured out what to do before introducing the girl to a frightening houseful of nuns and blind people. I saw now why it had taken her so long to come to the gate to greet me, and why the hem of her dress was wet. I imagined her wading into the lake, her sandals and socks left on the beach, to guide the Jewish girl's raft to shore, achieving in a breath what Thomas and I had spent our whole summer planning to do.

After the girl finally emerged from that pile of old clothes, we watched her eat the apple and another bun that Muriel produced from her jumper pocket. She barely knew what it meant that she'd made it all the way across the lake to Canada. Whoever had put her on that raft would be happy she'd made it here, we said. We told her this was a good place for her, and that she'd be safe from now on.

She looked like any other girl to me, which was odd to realize at first, with her braided hair and pudgy face, blue skirt crumpled up around her. I'd never seen a Jew before, let alone met one. If the films they showed us at school were to be believed, they were a rare and tragic race, a people to be mourned, an eternal symbol of man's cruelty to man. She stared at us with a look of suspicion and fear on her face, staring at Muriel's hands, then mine, and I saw by the way she studied us that she wasn't sure who the freak was here on this foreign shore and who wasn't—the girl whose hands looked like they'd been burned in a fire or me.

MY FATHER WAS SITTING on the front steps when I got home later that afternoon. I wanted to tell him about the Jewish girl. I was bursting with the news. I was happy for her, of course, terrified though she was, because she'd be safe now. But I was happy for my family, too. I thought this rescue might reflect well on us, at least partially, and I wanted him to come with me to Mercy House and help her understand that she'd be safe here in Canada. But he had news of his own now.

I didn't sit down beside him when he told me that our mother had left us. I stood facing him, still panting, and listened to what he had to say. She'd left first thing in the morning—I'd not noticed, so taken by the promise of seeing Muriel again—and by now she was halfway to Montreal to board the ship that would sail tonight for Bremen, Germany.

He held the note she'd left in his hand, the same wafer-thin blue stationery she used when she sent letters to my uncle. It was folded into thirds, and worn already where my father had been gripping it too tightly between thumb and forefinger. He told me what she'd written. I imagined there was more to the note than he was willing to share with me—maybe a second reason for her departure, something that a boy could never understand. But what he told me was this: she believed her absence would be the cure for what ailed us. It was her all along, she wrote—the reason we lived as we did, in shame and always fearful—and in leaving she would remove the stigma that hovered over us. It was her greatest gift to us. Without her we'd have a chance. He said she was wrong about that. She was trying to accept blame where there was just blind ignorance. "I don't know if you know that about your mother," he said, after letting this sink in. "We're supposed to suffer for the sins of others. She was always ready to do that."

He offered the note for me to read myself then. I refused. I didn't want it to be true. If I read it and saw that it was, I'd be denied the opportunity to pretend none of this was happening, or that they'd simply argued, as parents did, and that she'd gone away to a hotel for a night and would be back in the morning.

Thomas was upstairs stretched out on his bed, head in his hands, staring up at the model airplanes hanging from our ceiling. He already knew she was gone. I asked him what was going to happen now. He said he could see that she'd been saying goodbye for the past few weeks. He hadn't noticed, but he saw it now, the way she'd been talking to him about the future and how brothers should look out for one another. Twice in a week she'd told him that people have to make sacrifices for those they love. He hadn't thought much about it. It was just Mom in one of those sad moods that came over her.

Now I understood—that's what she'd been talking about on the front porch that evening weeks earlier. When she'd mentioned the word *ideals*. She'd been preparing me, leaving quiet hints as she collected her transit visa from whatever office, packing hardly anything. In this last sacrifice she'd suffered alone, determined to bring peace to her family.

NEXT MORNING I FOUND my father sitting at the kitchen table drinking tea from a clear glass when I came downstairs. He was already dressed in his suit and tie. He looked upset still, tired and drained by worry, but he was doing his best to meet the day. I sat with him. I liked it when he did that with me when I was sick or feeling lonesome. It was the first time in my life I recall understanding on some level that he needed me and my brother as much as we needed him.

"Don't ever think in absolutes, okay?" he said. "That's all I have to say. There's always something hopeful out there— something to strive for. She'll come back to us. She's not gone forever." And with that he pushed out from the table. "Now go get your suit on. And wake up that brother of yours. It's going to be a long day."

After breakfast, Thomas and I helped each other tie our ties the way we always did on Remembrance Day. We joined our father on the front porch shortly before ten-thirty. He straightened our lapels and said we looked right as rain, everything was going to be okay, we'd get through this one just like we always had. He adjusted his own tie, ran his hand through his hair, and moved his neck in that way he did when he wore the suit my mother had made for him too long ago.

We didn't talk at all on our way to Chisolm Square that morning. The day was warm, the sky cloudless. It felt strange that our mother was missing. I imagined her standing on the deck of the liner that would carry her to Europe, sailing through the Miracle Canal my father had helped dig.

All was familiar to me when we arrived at the park—the crowds gathering, the crackle of the public address system, the red-brick houses that fronted the space.

We found our customary spot among the small grouping of spruce trees at the north end of the square. At eleven sharp the service began. As usual the Reverend from Knox Presbyterian presided. His old hands shook as they always did; the pauses in his speech were long enough to cause concern. Every time he fell silent it seemed he might not start again, that this last word might have been his final breath as the script he held before him quivered in the light breeze. But he would rally and continue on until time came for the town dignitaries to come forth to place their wreaths at the base of the cenotaph. Some of them were seniors. Others were my father's age or slightly older, chief among them the veterans, of course—forty-year-olds who walked on one leg, or didn't walk at all, assisted by another whose wounds were not readily apparent. And then came the reading of the names.

My mind was still ringing with the fact that our mother was gone, and that, according to Thomas, she was gone forever. I didn't want to believe that. I wanted to believe some version of the story as told by our father. She'd be back, and soon enough. Maybe she'd help build bridges between us here in this country and people in Germany. Perhaps she'd act as emissary and return with news that they were not so different from us, or that they'd learned remorse and now sought forgiveness. Would there not be a new and wiser generation that had learned from the past? It felt odd to stand here beside my father without her. His arm, always linked with hers during the ceremony, rested solemnly at his side until he folded his hands across his waist.

Yet apart from these worrying thoughts and our mother's absence, the morning was as it always was at this point. The squirrel and bird chatter was hushed, as if in deference to the seriousness of the moment. The hard-rock granules and mineral filler in the black-shingled rooftops of the houses that fronted the square sparkled in the mid-morning sun. It might have been another fine summer day if it hadn't been the sixteenth anniversary of the bomb.

Now the Reverend rose from his seat beside the growing tribute of wreaths at the foot of the cenotaph to introduce the girls who were to read the names of those who'd died since the last memorial service.

This was when I saw her, the Jewish girl Muriel had rescued only the day before.

She stepped to the dais with the two other girls, her hair spilling out from behind her ears and resting on her shoulders in a delicate wave. The three of them wore identical cartwheel hats and long white dresses, white shoes, and a white ribbon tied on the left wrist. In the turmoil of what had greeted me when I got home the day before, I'd thought of nothing but our mother's leaving. Now, as the girl stood there holding the names of the recent dead she was to read, the Reverend told the crowd her story—that this child had been rescued on our shores and that she was a living embodiment of the injustice we'd all sworn to defeat. Here was a victim of the ignorance and prejudice that ruled so much of the world and that we must continue to resist. A chorus of "Amen" rose up. We stood rooted as the Reverend described the terrors she'd lived through.

The crowd grew agitated as he spoke. With each new detail of the conditions her family had lived under—the roving mobs, the forced evictions—they called out their insults and threats against the irredeemables among us. My father's hand fell to his side and searched out mine, as if he was preparing to pull me away. To our right, a few trees over, was the Schwabe family, Toby and his mother and father and older sister, each wearing the grim expression that, if Toby was to be believed, masked the doubt they carried in their hearts about the history that drew us here. I wondered what they thought about the girl up there now, if they would find some reason to disbelieve everything the Reverend told us about her.

The girls read the names when he finished speaking, and this seemed to settle the crowd back into sombre reflection. The Jewish girl's hands shook with nervousness but she didn't cry. Thirty-two new names were added to that sad list that year. She read out the last ten, stumbling on the foreign-sounding ones. Perhaps she was too young to understand what was being asked of her.

The minute of silence arrived at last and the world stopped, as if a hand had stilled the ticking of time. The fear and anxiety became more focused still and grew worse as the minute wore on. That's when the girl began to cry. Most eyes were cast downward, as mine should have been, but secretly I watched her and knew she was thinking about being alone now in this new world without her people. I wanted the girl to see me through the crowd. I wanted her to know that I'd nothing to do with putting her before this crowd like some sort of circus act. But she didn't look up. I was not able to ask forgiveness or to tell her that, despite the fact that I was German, I understood what she felt.

And then the ceremony was over. The sound of the ship-yard steam whistle split the air, ending our minute of silence, and we all saluted, a thousand families at once, and the crying girl was swallowed up by the milling crowd.

WE STARTED PREPARING THE house as soon as we got back, though I wondered if, for the fact that my mother was not here, we'd be granted some sort of grace, which of course had been her thinking all along. The depth of the sacrifice guaranteed it, I thought. They'd have got word of her leaving and they'd leave us alone. We'd sit nervously but unbothered at the kitchen table long into the night. But we prepared nonetheless. We changed into our street clothes and filled pots and pans with tap water and set them just inside the front door while our father soaked the lawn and the tree with the garden hose. Half a dozen curious onlookers were already gathering across the street. They chattered among themselves and nodded and paced back and forth. I watched them from the window the way my mother used to and imagined which one would throw what, and who carried the axe that would end up in our birch tree, and which neighbour would make it partway up our driveway or into our garage before our father scared him off with his baseball bat.

We waited at our kitchen table the way we always did, listening as the crowd grew. Everything was the same as it was every year, except that our mother wasn't here now. The single lit candle cast its glow over our faces. The main breaker in the basement was turned off. We'd set up the chessboard to pass the time. It was ignored in the end that night, as it always was. Also at the ready was the stack of comics Thomas and I might flip through while we waited for the crowd to thin. That's when I noticed the novel called *The Butterfly Cage* in the pile. I wondered if this meant Thomas knew of my visits to Mercy House and if he'd read the book about the poor girl trapped in that imaginary penal colony.

There was still light in the sky when the real crowd began to form. It was bigger and more determined than ever before; the crest of the wave we'd been expecting had arrived that day, and only added to the passions that had been inflamed by the living proof of the orphaned girl who'd spoken the names of the dead at the cenotaph that afternoon. Dozens of rafts had appeared as we'd paid our respects at Chisolm

Square. In a matter of hours the harbour had turned into a refugee aid station. Some were sick, most hungry, all of them dehydrated and bearing stories of what it was to live in a place like America where synagogues were torched, foreigners rounded up, and politicians spoke with admiration of the policies that had brought order to Europe.

We learned of this the following day as we surveyed what was left of our house. But that night we knew only that the crowd was wilder than it had ever been, and as the last light of day left the sky, the field across the road disappeared under a sea of people. The sound of bottles breaking on the driveway punctuated the chanting. *Eye for an eye! Eye for an eye!* The men out there were drunk—they were every year. It was a tradition now, like Christmas or Thanksgiving, a high mass in the season of mourning.

Our father watched from the window, slapping the bat gently against his open palm. Men appeared with fuel for the fire they'd build on our lawn. They stacked broken chairs and skids and bundles of newspaper, this time a whole picnic table, tree branches, and bags of garbage. The bonfire was lit as the crowd grew.

My mother wasn't here now to pester him back into his seat in the kitchen. Thomas and I joined him by the window. We saw the bonfire flames jumping as high as the lowest branches of the birch tree. It spread upwards and along the branches closer to the trunk. The night was fully dark now beyond the circle of light cast by the fire. The crowd tossed more fuel onto the flames and the fire moved freely, finding its fuel higher and wider throughout the tree until the whole thing was alight and the world seemed to be burning.

We begged him, as our mother used to, to stay close. The expression on his face showed anger now more than fear. It seemed he'd crossed over to some new understanding of what he was looking at, maybe something she'd always known and told him to recognize but he hadn't been able to until now. Things would never change here.

We didn't know the flames had leapt to the roof of our front porch, carried by sparks and burning branches, until we smelled the smoke coming from upstairs. From the roof the fire had rolled its way up and into the front room on the second floor. The bags of fabrics our mother used for the clothing she made for us were already in flames when we got up there, and the burning-hair smell of the prized angora wool she'd been saving filled the air. Coughing through the smoke, we ran up and down the stairs, buckets splashing and banging against our thighs, but it was clear we'd lost this fight. It was spreading too rapidly. We were panting heavily now. The air was too thick with smoke. Our father yelled to us that there was no saving the place, he just had to get a few things from his bedroom—some precious heirloom or document or money, I didn't know—but Thomas and I had to get out now. He pulled my brother in close to him and said something into his ear. Thomas nodded and took my hand and pulled me down the stairs and out the front door.

My eyes and lungs were burning, and outside the chanting of the crowd fell off as we dropped to our hands and knees on the driveway and retched. There were hundreds of people gathered now, so many that they spilled onto the road. Only the hardiest and most ardent of them moved about on the front lawn by the original bonfire.

We waited for our father to come out, kneeling there on the driveway like boys at prayer, watching the front door, the night lit by the fire. Thomas held my arm when I got up and called out towards the house. I called out again and again and tried to break free from my brother's grip but he did not let go. Smoke billowed from the windows, heavy and black, and poured up the side of the building. A pumper was there now and men set to work to bring down the flames. They told us to get back, far back, across the street. From there the night still felt hotter than an oven.

Thomas was still holding me by the arm but I was not struggling anymore. We watched the numbers painted on the front door bubble up and burn, and when the team of firefighters determined that the structure could not be rescued they turned their hoses on the trees and the houses on either side of ours.

The sound of the inferno roared on and turned the night sky bright as day. Cheers went up every time a part of the building collapsed in on itself.

The crowd grew larger still. Revellers gathered to watch the German house burn to the ground. Even now, these many years later, I cannot describe the heart of a child as he watches his life disappear before his very eyes.

IN THE MORNING ONLY the brick chimney remained standing. The crowd had thinned during the night but was collecting again. Men removed long planks from the back of a truck, sprayed them down with water, and laid them out over the foundation. The fire marshal arrived and held a white cloth to his mouth and nose as he walked along the planks inspecting the ruins. He'd stop every few steps and lean down to pick at something with the long pole he carried. Above what had once been our living room he shook his head and crossed himself, and Thomas took my hand and said we had to leave now, there was nothing left for us here.

The inevitability of our grief and hopelessness was close on us now, and soon it would leave us gutted and over-come with despair as the reality of our situation pushed itself into our hearts. But as my brother pulled me away I almost believed I heard our father's voice calling out to us—that he'd tricked fate somehow and found a way back out into the night as the house burned to the ground. It was a boy's desperate fantasy, a last attempt to hold on to the life that was gone now. I didn't hear that voice, of course. There would be no sudden reversal from the turn our lives had taken. I think Thomas knew this before I did. I'm sure of it. As he pulled me away from there, I heard him say again and again, "Don't look back, don't look back, there's some-where to go now," though in the state I was in—I was crying helplessly—I didn't think to ask where that somewhere was.

The streets were filled with people flowing in the direction of our house, small groups, families, gangs of boys excited to see what it was that had kept their fathers busy in the night. Smoke was heavy in the air. It hung over the street like scented curtains, blue and billowing in the early-morning light.

Just south of Chisolm Square we saw a crowd pelting a burned-out house with rocks and bottles. We couldn't read the number painted on the door—it had been melted by the heat—but it was clear that another German family lived there.

The riots weren't isolated to our town. We learned later that this night came to be known as Devil's Night for the spirit that had been unleashed across the country that eve-ning. But it was not the Jewish girl's story told by the old Reverend that had inspired the mob. It was the photograph published in papers around the world that showed the Amer-ican president shaking hands with Chancellor Göring after issuing the executive order that brought the Rademacher Act into full force. Trains and buses would soon begin delivering settlers (this, the official name) to ports of departure at New York, Savannah, Baltimore, Charleston, and Philadelphia.

By the fall of 1961 the deportations would be fully under-way. According to the act, the seizure of Jewish property would finance the clearances. The American taxpayer could rest assured, President Thurmond said, that the burden would be borne by the avaricious Jew. Within days of the executive order, shipping lines began the bidding for contracts to deliver their cargo to the Indian Ocean. It was to be a booming industry, as rich as oil, and might last a decade when all was said and done—such was the infestation to be dealt with.

We saw a body hanging by the neck from a tree beside the post office that morning. Thomas covered my eyes and told me to keep walking. But I'd seen the man's face, purple and bloated. It was Dieter Schwabe, Toby's father. We kept moving, to where I didn't know, and finally, just east of the harbour, we found a place down by the lake in among rocks the size of a man, placed there as a breakwater. No one would see us from the path above, my brother said. We were safe there. We'd rest until night fell. And then we'd do what our father had explained when he'd leaned into Thomas's ear last night before we left our burning house.

AFTER DARK WE WALKED to the fallout shelter hidden at the back of the Chisolm Allotments, just a few blocks from where we'd been hiding. This was where we needed to go, our father had told Thomas. He'd said it would be safe for us, and that we'd find there what we'd need. We heard gunshots and sirens going off but it was not possible to know what direction these sounds came from. In the glow of street lamps the smoky haze of our burning town swirled in the humid summer night. The allotment was wild with growth at this point in the summer. The swing-gate creaked as we entered and Thomas set it on its latch again once we were through. We walked along the narrow path that ran down the middle of the grounds between rows of plants. It was as quiet as a cemetery but for the gentle waves troubling the stones on the beach just down the hill. A half-moon sat low over Lake Ontario, and as I followed Thomas the plants brushed their dew-damp leaves against my legs and arms.

The entrance of the fallout shelter, set into the side of the hill that marked the eastern edge of the allotment, was an old wooden door encased in a cinder-block frame overgrown with climbing ivy. If you didn't know what it was you might have thought it was a place to store gardening tools, for the sign that read SHELTER 49, painted over the cinder block, was nearly invisible under the densely matted vegetation that hung there. This was one of the many shelters we knew about in town, though we'd never investigated this one in particular. The allotment was active three seasons out of four and people from this neighbourhood were always coming and going here, tending their plots; in wintertime the gate was kept locked.

When Thomas tried the door it resisted at first, as if something was barring the way on the other side. A second push opened it with a stuttering jump, and it scraped heavily against the door frame. Speaking into the darkness, Thomas asked quietly if anyone was there, and when there was no answer he stepped through and disappeared into the void.

I waited by the open door, listening for what was happening inside, afraid that he, too, would vanish from my life. I hated to be standing there, buckled over in loss. This was nothing that would ever get better. It was now who we were. In an instant we'd become orphans in the world. Our mother could not return from there, not the way things were. It was either Little Berlin for us now or one of the province's labour camps, a thought too miserable to bear as I waited there in the allotment for my brother. Like never before, as if the words themselves had no meaning until that moment, I knew their terrible weight and felt the permanence of my loss, helpless and alone. I was barely thirteen years old and yet I felt I'd been alive forever, as lonely and forgotten as a dying star in the night. I did what I could to guard my sobs, trying to listen for my brother's footsteps inside the shelter. I needed him. I needed someone. I cried for my father and for my mother, and for the life that had been ripped away from me, so quickly that it seemed it had never existed at all.

Thomas was gone longer than I could account for, or maybe it had been less than a minute, but now I saw a beam of light flicking deep inside the shelter. It moved towards me in short, jerking steps. I backed away from the entrance, and then his voice came through the darkness and finally he appeared again and told me it was safe, it was empty, and to follow him. He'd found a flashlight on one of the bunk beds that lined the walls. He flicked it on and off and directed the beam forward and side to side as he led me down the length of the shelter.

It was damp and mouldy-smelling, barely the width of a school bus, and reached far back into the hillside. It was more a tunnel than it was a room, all brick and bunk beds, long enough to house dozens of people, maybe even a hundred. A temporary shelter, it was nothing like those you could survive in for months, outfitted with water and basic foodstuffs and first-aid kits. The space was empty but for the wooden bunks; whatever provisions had once been there had been removed—looted, or reclaimed by the municipality, it was impossible to say.

"But the flashlight?" I said.

"It means someone was here. I know."

We moved deeper into the hillside down the length of the shelter, the light tracing over the brick walls in short, jerky movements, maybe fifty or so feet to the last bunk bed at the far end. This was where we'd be sleeping tonight, he said. Then we'd see. We'd wait and see. For what, he didn't know. He seemed as ignorant of our father's plans for us as I was. He'd delivered us to the shelter our father had told him to go to, but nothing more.

There was some clutter there at the back end of the shelter: gardening equipment for the allotment—rakes and shovels, buckets, a pickaxe, and an old wheelbarrow turned up against the wall. I tested the bunk and sat. There was no mattress, just a hard board.

Thomas took up a spade and walked back to the front of the shelter, the way our father did with the baseball bat he carried when he patrolled the house on those nights the crowds came. I wondered if anyone had followed us, and if my brother would be able to wield that spade the way he meant to suggest. He turned off the flashlight and creaked open the door and looked outside. The slightest sliver of light from the night sky drew his silhouette for me. I wanted him to come back into the far recesses of the shelter and to hear him tell me that our mother was going to be okay wherever she was, and that she'd track us down no matter what. I wanted him to snap his fingers to make all this go away. I wanted him to tell me that our father had gotten out of the house in time and that he'd come for us and lead us to safety.

The air in the shelter was cold and damp and the chill moved through me and set me to shivering. It was still warm outside, just on the other side of that door, but it was cold in there, and the wood of the bunk was cold too and smelled of earth and rot. Thomas closed the door again and walked back to where I sat on one of the bunks and said we needed to lie down and sleep now. I was too afraid and thirsty and hungry to sleep, I said. He sat down on the bunk beside me and put his arm around my shoulder and said he was afraid too, and we'd find something to eat and drink in the morning. We'd figure out what to do next. Maybe things would settle down in town and we'd be looked after. Maybe the worst of it was over. I knew he was saying this for himself as much as for me, and that he didn't really believe it, but it was all he could offer us, and I felt as bad for him as I did for myself. He knew he was supposed to take care of me. It was up to him now that our father was gone. I was his kid brother. He'd always looked after me, tried to take care of me in the schoolyard. Even when he'd thrown that salute to the German work crew, when the hatred in that moment had frightened me more than I'd ever been before, I saw myself in him, the hopelessness that was our life here and the frustration that finally spilled out in that desperate plea.

He got up then and climbed the ladder to the top bunk and settled in. The bedframe creaked. I imagined our father moving through the garden now to find us, arms loaded with supplies, and then the fantasy slipped away just as quickly as it had come. I would not meet my father at the gates of the Chisolm Shipyards again, or hear the sound of my mother's knitting needles clacking away in the living room while I worried through my homework. I tried to bring back the thought of our father coming to us, but what I heard instead was Thomas beginning to pray in the bunk above me. His words were mumbled and rushed between breaths. It was difficult to make out what he was saying to God but I knew this was a prayer because of the way he was talking to himself. He was quiet again for a time then, and I decided it might be a good idea if I prayed, too. I'd never really prayed before, not with any conviction, but I'd seen my mother do it, and I tried it now. I didn't raise my hands to my face, as might have been expected, but I prayed silently in my head, thinking anyone who might have the power to do something about what was happening would probably be able to hear without me having to say it out loud.

I don't know how long I'd been asleep when Thomas shook me awake and told me to listen, be quiet and listen. He was sitting on the bed beside me now, one hand on my shoulder, the other holding the flashlight, turned on and directed to the back wall of the shelter. He'd heard something, he said. He swung the flashlight beam over the wheelbarrow and the other gardening tools. It was just a lot of junk back there. My heart was beating like a fist. And then I heard it too.

He got to his feet, holding the light steady on the upturned wheelbarrow, and raised a finger to his lips. I was too frightened to speak as it was, though. Wide-eyed, I watched the wheelbarrow as the sound behind it grew louder. Thomas took the spade in hand and stepped closer to the back wall.

The wheelbarrow shifted, and then it slid sideways and fell to the ground. Where the barrow had stood was a small wooden door—a half-door, it seemed, with an old rusted knob. He held the light steady as the knob turned.

The door pushed open and a man's head appeared. He emerged and stood, nodded to us, and raised his hands as if in surrender. Thomas held the shovel against him, poised and at the ready. With his other hand he directed the flashlight beam from the stranger to the small door and back again, lingering on his face.

The man moved a hand to cover his eyes. "Yes, I'll tell you everything," he said in German. His clothes were covered in dirt, his hair thick and greying. "But we have to move fast."

1945

After Rosa died, Elser told Dr. Ridley that God had blinded him for a reason, and that he did not deserve the surgical procedure the doctor was offering. Use your talents on a worthier man, he said.

The opportunity was presented to him again three months later. He wanted nothing more now than to look into his daughter's eyes, he told the doctor, and forty-eight hours after the operation, the bandages were removed and there in a patch of October sunlight stood Ridley and two nursing sisters.

Elser rose from his bed and crossed the small room and looked at the Great Lake and wondered if he still wasn't half-blind, the far shore so distant as to be unseen. He wondered at the clarity of the sky and the gulls that hung in it, such elegant, simple things. He embraced the doctor and the two sisters, who blushed at his exuberance. In his broken English he complimented the doctor on this miracle. And then he crossed the lawn to the great house in his hospital gown to look at his daughter for the first time in his life.

LINA TEUFEL WAS IRONING bedsheets in the laundry room when he appeared. The bassinet was placed on a work-table across from her. She watched him pick up his daughter and stare at her. For a moment she failed to understand that he was looking at his child, actually seeing her for the first time. He seemed different, but the understanding came as an echo returned to her with some slight pause. She knew the surgery had happened, yet for a moment she was puzzled at the sight of what she believed was a blind man staring at a thing with such intensity that he seemed overwhelmed to the point of tears. And then she understood. She put her hand over her mouth and shook her head in wonder, and she too cried for the miracle that this was.

IT DID NOT TAKE long after that for the secrets to begin to fall away. First, the shared language. Lina and Elser walked the grounds and spoke in hushed tones, careful that the late-autumn breezes did not betray their confidence. They fell silent again when a sister or Dr. Ridley appeared. At first their walks were not commented on. But then Sister Evelyn hinted at suspicions that had taken root among the staff and residents. *Fraternization* was not the word she used, but it was implied well enough. Such a thing was not tolerated here. Elser understood this, yet every morning he looked forward to her arrival and the walk they took together in the garden once the baby was fed. He often met her at the gate, his daughter cradled in his arms, and when the child saw the wet nurse she reached for her, drawn by the smell of milk. Lina Teufel took her now without fear or reluctance.

Sometimes she sang to the child in German when the three were alone. She told him of her life outside the gates and about the town that hated people like them, and about her son, Thomas, not much older than this one here, she said, condemned to suffer for the sins of others. She spoke of her husband, too—his steady employment at the shipyard and his good nature and how, without him, half-German and Canadian-born, she would have been sent to the camp that blighted the north end of Port Elizabeth. She told him about her old life in Germany and the crossing on board the *St. Louis* and the camp in the Azores. The retelling of her ordeal moved him, not for the hardship she described but for the crimes against her that she didn't talk about. The sorrow he felt in hearing her story and knowing the terrors she'd lived through opened his heart to her. It was pity at first, and compassion, and, foolish man that he was, he slowly began to feel something more.

He had no other word for it. He said it aloud for the first time into his daughter's ear. *Is this old fool father of yours in love?* he asked. *Has the gift of sight blinded me so?* The wet nurse's smile cheered him from his routine in a way that amazed him; he fell off to sleep recalling their conversations, and how she gazed over the lake when they walked behind the house, the look on her face at once so familiar and profound that he thought he'd known her his whole life. The ease with which they spoke as they strolled the grounds that season came not only due to the language they shared. It was much more than that by now, he knew; but he knew too that this was a foolish game he permitted himself. It would go no further than to ease the mourning he still endured. He was, in the end, nothing if not a realist, a practical man. Yet he allowed this to feed him the measure of hope that would carry him forward, and this in and of itself might also have been the result of some practical concern for survival—this need to look forward with something more than despair in one's heart.

He would involve himself in the care of those around him now that his sight had been restored. He could be useful to the sisters as they tended to their daily chores. Whatever they needed from him he would provide. It was a gesture towards penance, of course, and an added layer to his camouflage as a Dutchman among these survivors. But this was also the sort of self-preservation that a man like him required. Without work or purpose he was nothing, and so he applied himself. While the wet nurse cared for his daughter, he assisted with the various patients who'd become bedridden since their arrival, lifting and bathing, and he helped unload the delivery trucks that rolled in. With a population nearing one hundred, there was no lack of things to be tended to.

It did not occur to him that he'd be asked to leave soon, now that he was sighted again and, unlike so many others there, had not been taken by one of the cancers they saw so much of. As Julius DeGroote, he would be free to go. More than this, he was expected to go. Where to he had no idea. Into town, he supposed, to work with men at the shipyard perhaps, or to Hamilton where the Stelco Company stoked the fires whose distant glow lit those cool autumn nights.

He was resolved. In early December he prepared to be turned out. He'd been given tours of the town and introduced to potential employers in need of a labourer or assistant, a plumber's helper or carpenter's apprentice. There would be opportunity, they assured him, and through their wide network of charities the sisters helped him find a place to stay and a woman, herself widowed, to look after the child while he gained employment and worked to better his situation. He made his rounds and said his farewells, and on his last evening at Mercy House, before the wet nurse was to leave, her long day finally ended, she found him in the makeshift nursery putting his daughter down for the night.

He was gentle and loving with the child now. Perhaps he'd learned from her example, she thought. She was pleased to see that a man so scarred by the war might still find love in his wounded heart for that poor child. He laid his daughter in her crib and sang to her quietly.

Lina took his hand and held it as a wife might do, or so it seemed to him, without shame or hesitation but simply with the easy trust of those bound by the shared love of a child. He felt the warmth of her face near his as she leaned in to watch the baby drift off, eyes closed now. It was a small moment, this one added to the many they'd shared these last months. His admiration for her had grown as they continued on in the project of caring for the child. And now came the quickening in the heart that was the illusion of youth, and then just as suddenly it was gone, and he forced himself back towards the proper demeanour that was expected of the circumstances that bound them.

HE STOOD OVER HIS wife's modest grave the following afternoon to say goodbye. The falling snow softened the trees and the hard earth in the woods far behind the consecrated grounds of the chapel cemetery, where those who'd sinned against God were not welcome. Here she would remain, in this small clearing, with a view to the lake she'd never seen. He wondered if she could see it now, somehow, in the mystery of death, and the flat, carved stone that marked this place as hers. Behind him stood the wet nurse and Dr. Ridley and Sister Evelyn, come to pay their last respects as this couple was finally parted, Rosa DeGroote to remain there forever, and the widower who'd carry their child out into the world.

He felt chastened and ashamed and thrilled by the power of the emotions that had taken him as he'd held Lina's hand. An old fool, after all was said and done, he thought.

It was a poem that came to him unbidden as he stood there, and at once Sister Evelyn and Dr. Ridley turned their heads to him, as if he'd just then performed some marvellous bit of magic. At first they thought they'd heard wrong. But they'd heard perfectly well. They didn't know what poem it was, but its meaning was of no importance. It was the language he spoke it in, the words to the piece of music his mother had often sung to him when he was a child, and that he'd heard the night he was detained at the Swiss border all those years ago. It came to him freely, like a man speaking in tongues, and at once they understood that a German had been living in their midst this whole time.

1960–1983

I thought I saw something in the man's eyes that told me he was sorry for what had happened to our father, though of course I couldn't know this as we stood there in the fallout shelter that night. He'd lowered his hands slowly and called us by our names and told us in German that he'd take care of us now, we were safe with him. He waited a moment for us to say something. But we just stood there, both of us too frightened and shocked to say anything at all. He was a complete stranger to us and to our family's history, as far as we knew, crawled up from a hole in the middle of the night—until he told us that he'd known our father for years, since we were small, and that it was our father who'd arranged for this meeting.

He was to be our guide tonight and for the weeks to come, he said, and right now we were to climb into the tunnel and follow his every instruction, no questions asked. Thomas was to go first, he said, then me. He'd follow behind so he could seal the door properly.

The doubt and shock I'd seen in Thomas's face began to fade as he pieced this together in his mind. What our father had said to him as we'd prepared to leave our burning house the night before was coming clear. This was what our father had arranged. To meet this man. This was the help he'd promised we'd find at Shelter 49.

Thomas got down into a crouch, flashlight shining ahead, and disappeared into the hole.

I followed him, too afraid not to, and crawled after the light that marked his progress.

The tunnel was only just wide enough for one person at a time to pass through it; the earthworks overhead and along the sides fell in clumps here and there as I moved on hands and knees. I heard the door shut behind me, our guide closing the three of us in, and there was just enough light from the flashlight he carried to see Thomas a few body-lengths ahead of me. It wasn't far, maybe twenty feet away, that the exit came into view.

I wanted to get myself out of that cramped space, but I was afraid of what we'd find at the other end. I saw the small circle of light that was the opening, meaning Thomas was through now, and then a moment later I was through too.

I got to my feet in a room of arched brick walls and wooden benches and bunks similar to the ones we'd slept on in the allotment shelter we'd just cleared out of. A single bulb was strung from the ceiling by a black wire. Thomas was facing away from me, staring at something.

I had no idea what was above us, but I knew the name of the girl he was staring at, standing at the far end of the shelter, and what it was about her—apart from the fact that there was someone else down here—that had captured his attention.

It was Muriel's hands that held his gaze, of course, and when the man emerged from the tunnel a moment later he told us to stop gawking at one another and to get a move on, there'd be time enough for explanations later.

Muriel and I didn't speak as our guide led us along a narrow corridor into another cellar, this one smaller than the last. We didn't stop there. Thomas and I traded looks as we walked. I don't know what he saw in my eyes. Confusion, mostly likely, and a fearful anticipation of what waited for us around the next corner. That's what I saw in his eyes, at least—that and the need to know who this girl was. It had been shocking enough to meet her in the light of day. Now, in this strange underworld, he might have set to hunting for an explanation for who and what she was. It was not clear how, if at all, these two were related, our guide and the girl with the claw-like hands, or where he was leading us. But there was no turning back, that much I knew. Any logic to the design and layout of the passageways we travelled through was lost on us after the first few turns. It would have been impossible to find our way back to where we'd started.

There were offshoots and side chambers where tunnelling equipment was stored—shovels and planking and wheelbarrows. The passageway we followed was lit by bulbs strung from the wooden support beams that crossed overhead every fifty feet or so, and soon, as the passageway narrowed, by lanterns set on shelves carved into the dirt wall.

Sharp turns came out of nowhere. Three times I could have sworn we'd looped back around again in the direction we'd started from. There were dips and rises in elevation, and twice we came upon stairs carved into the earth that took us deeper still. The air was stale and cold and set a shivering over me that I couldn't control. I walked, arms wrapped around myself, teeth chattering, wondering if this was really my life or some stranger's nightmare I'd stumbled into. Our guide was out front, just a few steps ahead of Muriel. Thomas was behind me.

The man traded his flashlight for a lantern he'd taken from one of the chambers we'd passed through. It cast a yellow glow over the walls of the tunnel as he moved forward, and when the path ahead curved and the roughed-out walls seemed to bend there always came a moment when I felt certain we'd see someone emerge from the darkness, waiting for us. I didn't know who that would be but it was always a terrifying prospect. I thought of the Citizen Patrol or any of the vigilantes who'd be roaming above ground now, searching for more Germans to lynch. But for now only the darkness we moved towards waited for us as we kept on, marching endlessly through that series of tunnels, shivering and unsure of our next step.

Water dripped from the dirt ceiling and the ground grew soft with puddles that were too big to step over. The wooden support beams bent under the weight of the earth above. We were under the lake now, or maybe the Burnt River, but our guide was too far ahead to ask in a quiet voice, and I worried that any sound above a whisper might bring the tunnel down on our heads.

There had always been rumours about the Germans who disappeared, the camp-dwellers or the families who'd been allowed to live in town among the regular citizens, as we had been—a whole family gone overnight, houses empty the next day, as if no one had lived there in the first place. This wouldn't be the first time people like us had travelled through this maze, and I wondered if this was an offshoot of the Underground Railroad that had delivered men and women to our town and towns like it along the north shore of Lake Ontario a hundred years earlier, and if by some strange reversal it was now the path that would carry us in the opposite direction, away from our torment and persecution.

The ugly fact that we were German meant we'd be free in America, welcomed into the heart of the nation that had terrified my father. It was the blood in our veins that would speak for us, and as this reasoning came clear to me I wondered if this was what my brother had wanted all along, to go to America—with our parents, not with just me, not under these terrible circumstances—to end up in a place where we'd not only be accepted but privileged for our race and heritage. The salute he'd given the work gang onboard that truck as they'd passed through our sleeping town might have been a first sign of some long-shifting allegiance that would finally find its full expression there, and I felt more trapped and helpless than I ever had, a slave to my fate and the ideals our father had tried to instill in us.

We emerged into the night air at the foot of a hill over-looking the lake after three or four hours down there in those miserable tunnels. I was exhausted, my feet were sore and wet, but it felt good to breathe fresh air again. We drained the water from our shoes and wrung out our socks and rested for a short time, and slowly the warm summer night took hold again and the shivering fell away. Out on the lake a flotilla of twenty or thirty ships was lit by the half-moon that had illuminated the allotment we'd passed through ear-lier that night. It had leapt westward in the sky, I could see, marking the hours we'd spent underground.

I got a clear look at our guide for the first time since he'd emerged from that door in the shelter. He was older than my father by twenty years or so and had deep lines in his face and sad, intelligent eyes that roamed among the three of us as we sat there, confused and frightened. My brother asked him to tell us what was going on, where he was taking us. "And who's this?" he said, meaning Muriel. "We don't know you. Either of you."

It's here the night's strange events began to make sense to me. The man identified himself not only as our guide that night but as our guardian, too, and said that our welfare was as much his responsibility as was the welfare of his own daughter. Muriel didn't seem to react at all when he turned to her as he said this. It was a surprise only to me and to Thomas, not at all to her, and in a moment the last two months dissolved before my very eyes. Everything I'd seen and thought and felt about her, it was all recast now. She was not an orphan, she was not alone. Here before us sat father and daughter, and now the orphan was me.

She did not attempt to hide behind the remoteness she'd met me with that first day at Mercy House. Now she was tired and undone, as much as Thomas and I were. She didn't care to explain herself or to hide her hands when it was clear my brother was staring. As for Thomas, he might have begun to understand that she was the person who'd seen us from the window at Mercy House after the Russian inspector blew his cigarette smoke over my cut hand. He would piece it together soon enough if he hadn't by now.

Muriel's father got us up and moving again, now in the direction of the gravel road not far from where we'd come up from the tunnel, where we waited until a truck came around the bend, headlights cutting the darkness.

We stood off in the trees and waited after it came to a stop, and when its headlights flicked off and on three times, Muriel's father stepped out from our cover and spoke to the man through the driver's-side window. He waved for us to come out, and we piled into the back of the pickup and were driven over a series of country roads that rang with the sound of calling crickets. The half-light of the waning moon shimmered on the dusty leaves of the trees at the side of the road, and when the bush cleared and the open pasture came into view we saw horses in a field, swinging their heads in the grey light.

It was maybe four in the morning when the truck left us at the edge of Hamilton Bay, overlooking the red glow of the Stelco furnaces. We watched the coke ovens throwing a sun's worth of sparks into the night. The air smelled of petrol and burning rock and iron.

There was water waiting for us in a satchel hanging from a tree branch Muriel's father knew to look for. The satchel carried bread, too, but no one was interested in food yet. We passed the water among us and eventually broke off chunks of bread from the loaf and sat without speaking until we saw something begin to move on the other side of the bay.

It was still too dark and too far away to understand what we were seeing, but after a time the crane and the long line of railcars heavy with slag came clear, and we saw the crane manoeuvre its claw and tip the house-sized loader buckets that sat on the car beds. One by one, the buckets were emptied and the molten slag, glowing like lava, spilled its orange burst of light down the hillside to the slurry pit of the bay, where it met the water in an eruption of steam that rolled upwards to the sky in great roiling clouds.

The sound came a moment later, like a thunderclap after a flash of lightning. It split the night, and the air around us was alive with light and sound as the bay boiled and the slag spilled down the hill, one enormous bucket after another. Before the last one was emptied we felt mist falling over us like a light rain as we sat in the trees eating our bread and watching the world burn.

Muriel's father led us to a shallow cave close by when we heard the voices echoing up through the trees. It was almost light now. After we slipped into the rock shelter he raised a finger to his lips and nodded, but we would not have said a word for the fear that gripped us.

The men were near. We heard their voices coming from where we'd sat just moments before, though too far off to understand what they said or even to know how many of them there were, and finally the sound of the voices faded, tracking off downhill towards the bay.

UNTIL DARK WE WERE not allowed to wander more than a few steps from the rock we were camped under. It was too dangerous. More patrols might be out, Muriel's father said. Which meant we'd sit through the day with nothing to do but dwell on our hunger and thirst and boredom and, worse yet, the reality that our father was dead and there was no reason to believe we'd ever see our mother again. She'd been swallowed up by the amnesty as sure as our father had been swallowed by the smoke and the fire we'd only barely escaped.

Muriel now seemed to know what had happened to our family—her father would have told her in the hopes of explaining Thomas's silence and the sobbing that overcame me as I sat staring out across the bay. She did what she could to distract us from feeling the way we did, and though she was not much older than me, and the same age as my brother, she did her best to corral us away from our thoughts, at least for short periods while we waited to set out again.

She made us each a small sculpture of a butterfly using twigs for the body and antennae, and for the wings the whirlybirds that spun down and drifted into our rock shelter from the maple branches nearby. It was a small diversion but I was thankful for it, as was my brother. We collected our own twigs and maple keys and watched how it was done. Already the strangeness of her hands didn't seem to bother Thomas. If he hadn't figured out where she was from before that, he did now when she told us that one of the sisters at Mercy House had shown her how to do this when she was little.

AFTER DARK FELL, A young man carrying a walking stick and canteen appeared at the mouth of the shallow cave. We followed him through the woods to an old, beaten-up truck parked in a clearing just off a gravel road. We climbed in the back and drove for close to an hour to the edge of an orchard, where we waited, eating peaches we pulled from the trees, until a man and his shepherd emerged from the darkness. It might have been close to midnight by then. The sounds of crickets and the smell of fruit rotting in the grass filled the night.

The glow of the Stelco fires was behind us now. We saw them from the hill we climbed when we cleared the orchard. We'd travelled south. From there the fires were small in the distance.

This man took us into his home and gave us sandwiches and potato salad and apple juice at his kitchen table. I was determined not to think about what lay ahead, only about the meal in front of me. The man leaned against the countertop and watched us as we ate. He was a big, bald man named Avrahm who wore horn-rimmed glasses and had the name *Babette* tattooed on his left forearm. Afterwards he led Muriel's father into the backyard, where they spoke in whispers. I watched them from the kitchen window and imagined that my mother was sitting at the table behind me, knitting, counting stitches, or spinning wool the way she used to, and that my father was setting up the chessboard in the next room, getting ready to beat me the way he always did. I turned from the window, so taken by the hope, almost expecting her to be there with me, but only Muriel and my brother were there, hovering over their empty plates.

THE GUIDES WE MET as we travelled south along that
network of tunnels and roads and rest stops told us of the
chaos we'd escaped. The second wave of refugees had hit our
town two days after we'd left Port Elizabeth. They'd flooded
our streets and parks and slept in church basements and in
the auditorium of our school. The arson and lynching had
gone on for days, until there wasn't a German left in town.
Little Berlin had been burned to the ground.

Most of the refugees coming north had escaped by water,
as we'd predicted, but some came overland, too. We'd effected
no one's rescue in the end, my brother and I, and failed to
benefit from the wave of Jewish fugitives as we'd hoped.

We saw signs of the exodus everywhere, as they must have
seen of ours—cold campfires, tin cans, fresh initials carved
into a tree—and on our fourth night on the road Muriel's
father finally managed to tell us his story.

We were set up in the woods just east of North Pelham,
tired and hungry after walking through the night, the early
morning hovering at the edge of the trees. He told us about
the assassination and the labour camp and his escape to Holland, and about the day he met Muriel's mother on the *Eendracht* and the months they'd lived in a church in a London
suburb after they'd fallen blind. We'd seen pictures of these
evacuation centres and the blind survivors waiting to board
hospital ships bound for Canada and other points in the
Commonwealth. And we knew about the assassination, too,
of course, but little about the man behind it. He'd seemed

to disappear from the story, the events that followed erasing the very individual who'd triggered them, like a magician who vanishes into thin air at the height of his powers. And now here he sat, fully realized and connected to us in a way that hardly seemed possible. I was used to believing what adults told me, and more often than not what I heard from them was some unpleasant truth they felt I might not stumble upon without their help. Which was certainly the case now. Suddenly he was someone to be feared and respected—a man who'd done and suffered more than I could in ten lifetimes—and the idea of what awaited us at that point, under the guidance of such a man, sent my imagination on a frightening tear.

It seemed Muriel knew most of this story already, though. There was no look of surprise on her face as she sat staring into the campfire. She was beyond that, I think, with most of the facts already before her. But I wonder now if she was on the edge of understanding some newly revealed essential truth about the absences that had defined her life, and that these terrible circumstances that surrounded her might reverberate in some secret corner of her being for all time.

THE FOLLOWING DAY THE four of us crossed the Niagara River on a rowboat called the *Molly Bloom* piloted by a man who spoke with an Irish accent. He had a heavy growth of white beard and a broken hand wrapped in blue cloth, though he refused to let Muriel's father take the oars when he offered. There was a fog over the river that morning that rendered the light a dull pearl grey. The current was slow and steady, pulling us in a way the oarsman had to correct for, and when he landed us on the other side he passed me a rucksack of supplies that he said would hold us for two or three days. Without another word, he pulled away from the shore again, swung the boat around, and started back. I watched him disappear into the fog and thought how strange it was that he was rowing home now, all the while facing backwards.

ONCE WE CROSSED OVER into America, we travelled with a group of men and women sympathetic to our cause. From them we learned of the deportations that were already underway in the eastern states, targeting the Jews and everyone else who didn't belong, they said. Muriel's father told us that we were not headed for the America we'd been taught to fear but to somewhere out west, one of the sanctuary states or cities in the part of the country that had held out, rejecting federal immigration and race policies.

In mid-September we followed a group of Hasidic Jews, grateful for their numbers but fearful, too, that they'd discover our background and take their revenge on us. We camped at a distance from them, watching their fires, and in the morning when we broke camp we followed. The group consisted of five families, perhaps not so unlike my own, broken and grieving. On the seventh day a man from the group approached our camp with bread and sat with us and told us in detail of the place they were headed. Every port of the eastern seaboard was now gearing up for the project they were fleeing, he told us, but in the west there was still hope.

We stayed with them for weeks, on through Pennsylvania, Ohio, and Indiana, until they were discovered and taken by one of the bands of men who claimed them as bounty. Jews were worth more than we were, five dollars a head. Barely worth their time, we were questioned, race and origin verified, and lectured on the hazards of the Jew. We travelled hundreds of miles by foot and car and rail, skirting towns, avoiding checkpoints and race-hunters. Sometimes Muriel's father left us in camp for days, one time for so long that we believed he'd abandoned us or died, but on the fifth day he returned with new shoes for the three of us, a newspaper, a compass, food, and chocolate bars. We hid in an abandoned cabin and ate our fill, and slept, woke up, and ate some more, and when we'd eaten enough that we could easily carry what remained we set out again. We stole what we could and met fewer guides as we moved west. Head for Emporia, they'd say, and after a week or more a man in Emporia would bring us blankets and a pot of stew in his barn and tell us to keep on for Wichita, Great Bend, and then Dodge City.

We rode trains like hoboes in the pictures we'd seen of the Great Depression, but avoided those rail lines that

seemed to attract other freight-hoppers. These were the lines
that attracted the attention of the deportation agents and
race-hunters, who knew to look there for their quarry. We
took the secondary feeder lines that often carried us north
and south more than west, but west eventually, inching ever
closer to the sanctuary state we'd heard spoken of. The search
for Jews widened in the compliant states we passed through,
as one race law after the next was passed in the American
Congress and President Thurmond won his third term. We
read this in the newspapers Muriel's father returned with
after his solo trips into Mason City, Sioux Falls, and Faith,
where he watched dozens of Cheyenne line up in front of the
town hall to register for the fate that awaited them.

We walked through the month of October, and into the
second week of November we arrived at the mountain state
where big cats rustled the early-evening brush and bears
caught your scent from a mile off. The river at McCredie
Springs looked nothing like the river that cut through Port
Elizabeth. It was clear and fast and drew us to its banks, the
Jews and the others we lived among. We drank from it and
took its fish and carried it in jugs to our tents and cabins up
the side of the valley. Muriel's father helped construct the
small frame homes that needed to be built for those who
continued to arrive there, drawn to the sanctuary state of
Oregon by rumour and promise as the turmoil in the eastern states grew. With each new arrival reports came, none of
them hopeful. We were a growing community, ours and the

hundreds of others scattered over these mountains and all down the watershed to the Pacific Ocean.

NOW THOMAS AND I take fugitives down the McKenzie River on the last leg of the journey into Eugene, where we stay for a day or two before the long hike back to Clear Lake up here in the Willamette forest. We know the whitewater rapids well, and where the hidden boulders lie, the river's dangerous chutes and cascades. There have been a number of near-misses. We've lost a raft, more than a few backpacks, and any sense that we're in control when it comes to this beautiful cut of landscape. But we've never seen any serious injuries. The eighty-odd miles down will take us two days, three in July and August when the river's low, and triple that for the hike back up over the trails, each with the fifty pounds of supplies we never return without.

I cannot provide a fair or sensible assessment of my brother's character, such as it was back when we were boys. What he saw around us in those days was confinement and abuse, and he believed that those who suffered in the same way he did must be his friends and allies. His anger was his attempt to protect us from those who ruled our lives. When that truckload of German workers rolled past that night, he saluted those who knew our situation as intimately as we ourselves did, nothing more. We've never spoken of that night since then, or about the night our father died, but it might be true that brothers who lose their parents too soon will find a way of communicating without really talking, or maybe that's just the fantasy of young men who still believe that the things we think and feel are of no interest to anyone but ourselves.

I visit Muriel's father sometimes at Clear Lake, where he still lives in the cabin the four of us shared until Muriel went down to San Jose at the age of twenty-one, where she works in a residential care home for the blind. I try to bring things from the city for the old man—a can of peaches in syrup will still put a smile on his face—and with me he shares what news he has about his daughter. She enjoys her work with the children she cares for. Only weeks ago she took a group on an excursion to the Sierra Azul, he said, and learned the names of wildflowers she'd never known existed. I know by now he considers her to be the one good thing to have emerged from the tragic history that defines him. I see it in his eyes as he tells me what he knows, the stack of her letters to him bound by loose twine and set on the table by the wood stove.

He's in his eighties now. On Remembrance Day, if his legs are strong enough, I'll take him down to Belknap Springs and stand beside him in the small gathering that collects to commemorate the day. Brief and reverent, it's nothing like the ceremonies I remember from the days of my youth. Afterwards we shake hands with the men and women I recognize from our early days here, many of whom I've known since we arrived twenty-three years ago—the blacks and the

Jews and the Tillamook and the race- and gender-defiers. We are, as far as they know, just another broken family of refugees. None of them knows Elser's story. To them he is the old man who years ago appeared with three children in tow and managed to raise them well enough, despite everything.

They ask me what it's like in Eugene these days. They know I am one of the river guides who deliver refugees down to the coast. I tell them what I know, that things are going to get worse before they get better, and then the old man and I take the long hike back along the river to the cabin, where we'll prepare a modest supper of rice and beans and read by candlelight until it's time for bed.

Sometimes the day will have shaken loose a memory—a moment spent with my mother or father all those years ago—that he needs to share. There's nothing more he needs to tell me about them. I know what I need to know. But I can still enjoy a fresh image of my mother as she might have appeared to him on a certain day. He's been moved to go deeper into his past on a number of occasions, into his own childhood and memories of his mother and father, and once to talk about watching the clouds roll by as he lay feverish and near-dead on a coal barge on the Rhine River.

With time our losses fade and heal over, no matter how great they are, or how deeply they altered our lives. This is what I might have thought if I had not known Georg Elser. I might have thought that anguish and grief turn to sorrow and mourning, and that mourning slowly opens the memory to the gradual fading of the thing itself. I can say with some conviction that I am who I need to be, and who I should have been all along, despite the story I've lived. Isn't this the proper way of things?

But for the old man, I don't think so. I can't say what he feels on the matter of love and loss, and on the nature of the life he's led. What does a man like him feel as he nears the end of his days? I wondered this for years when I finally began to understand that guilt must be borne in solitude. It took me time to see that madness was never far off for him. Often he'd disappear for days at a time in the years following our arrival here, to where we never knew, until once, at the age of seventeen or eighteen, I followed him into the forest.

It was a full-day hike at the end of which I watched him stand for hours at the edge of a cliff until it was too dark for me to see him. What thoughts troubled his mind as he stood there I can't say. But at any moment he was a man poised to disappear over the edge. What surprises me now was that I did nothing. I watched and waited, far back in the trees, for him to jump or to step back from the edge.

That's when I understood that guilt is a form of madness when a good man's life brings little more than suffering and tragedy. I might tell him that the life he's lived was the life that he was born into and was supposed to live, and that he changed nothing that wasn't meant to be changed. That there is no history other than the one sad history we know. But I spare him the platitudes. He is beyond consolation.

Occasionally the imagined sound of my mother's knitting needles clacking away in the pine trees outside the window reaches my ear when I sit up late after he's fallen into his troubled sleep, and for a moment she's with me the way she used to be, quiet but there, before her own great sacrifice, fruitless and irreversible, took her away from us.

The mind reaches helplessly for what once was, after so much has been lost.

EPILOGUE

My mother had mentioned the white birch tree in our front yard more than once to Elser, that there was none other like it on the whole street. I watched the light of the fire playing over his face while he told us this part of his story that last night before we crossed the river to America.

He'd found the house after he spoke German over his wife's grave. It was just as my mother had described it to him, the birch tree standing there, glowing in the light of the December moon. He saw it well before our family identification number painted on the door came into view, and then he knew there could be no doubt this was her home.

He waited on the sidewalk until she came to the window, and a moment later my father stepped out onto the front porch carrying a rucksack. The two men shook hands, still strangers to one another.

There were provisions in the bag, my father told Elser, not much, but enough for a day or two. And then my father guided him to the shelter recessed into the hill at the foot of the Chisolm Allotment, from which point Muriel's father would lead us to safety almost fifteen years later.

This was when my mother understood that my father was involved in helping men like Elser escape to the sanctuary states in America. For months by then he'd been meeting with this group of partisans who assisted fugitives in any way they could. Later, after the first riots swept the town in 1953, following the news of the hydrogen bomb test in Libya, they'd talked about leaving as well. But it was too dangerous then, Muriel's father told us that night, and Thomas and I were too small to travel, practically babies still.

That night in the shelter, in December 1946, my father introduced Elser to the group who'd help get him over the border. They were people who'd been able to escape after being found in possession of a map of the province, or a German-language Bible, or having defied in some other way one of the hundreds of statutes that regulated our lives. The sentencing was harsh and swift—property confiscated, families split up and sent off to faraway work camps. Those who could went underground to join the resistance and moved by night beneath the town through the tunnels that fed its hopeless trickle on into distant America.

In the weeks to come Muriel's father stayed underground. He learned the tunnels and met with men and women as they waited their turn to be taken over the border, where they could begin the journey that awaited them.

My father visited him with updates on the search for the German who'd been processed into Mercy House under an alias. They had no idea who he really was, as far as my father could tell, he said. My parents were questioned over a period of weeks after he left, but they had nothing more to offer. The sisters isolated my mother from the other atonement girls at the hospice. There was discussion regarding the placement of the child. Some of the sisters wanted it gone, but most of the residents had charity in their hearts. The child would stay on, Sister Evelyn declared, and the nursing would continue.

Elser set out for the border the day after my father told him that his daughter would stay in my mother's care at Mercy House. Now at least she'd be well looked after. It took six days to reach the border, and when he stood on the bank of the Niagara River and watched the opposite side, wondering if he was capable of leaving his infant daughter forever, he knew his fight was there, back in the direction from which he'd just come.

He looked up from the campfire we were gathered around as he told us this. That was when he understood, he said, standing at the river's edge those many years ago. And in four nights he walked the hundred-odd miles back to Port Elizabeth, where, over the seasons that followed, he waited and watched Muriel from the rocky beach below the house and from the road outside the gates where Thomas and I had stood on so many occasions.

We never saw him, not once. I look back through my memory but I don't see him. He was there, he assured us, and with my mother's help he held his daughter in his arms once or twice a month through the ironwork of the gates, while my mother looked over her shoulder to make sure none of the sisters were watching. After her service of atonement was complete, she submitted a formal request to make the child her own. The sisters rejected the idea as perverse, but allowed her to visit on occasion. He'd been watching on that July morning—from where he didn't say—when I walked through the front gates of the Mercy House estate and met Muriel for the first time. With my mother's help he'd kept her in his life, and so when he came for Muriel on the night my father died, she knew to follow him.

He told us this last detail as we stood on the American side of the Niagara River the morning we crossed over. It was one of the few happy days in his life, he said, when he saw me pass through the gate and walk up the lane, knowing that I'd finally meet Muriel.

Standing on the muddy bank, I felt the weight of my circumstances for the first time. I wasn't ready until that moment, I suppose, to accept the reality of what awaited two teenaged brothers tossed up in the sort of storm that had turned our lives upside down. I was too young to understand the full breadth of the changes that were upon us—that would come later, as the months and years piled on—but on that morning I felt that the world was founded on a lie, and that the small part of it that our parents had occupied was a sort of grace afforded to us that we, in our ignorance and in the rush of youth, had been unable to recognize and to appreciate. I assign no blame here. We were children in difficult times. We loved them in the only way we knew how, in our own small selfish ways.

An opening in the fog drifted by as I listened to the oars somewhere out on the river. And then I saw the man again—the bandaged hand, the rough beard, the oars rising and falling like a heron's wings—and for an instant before the fog swallowed us up for the last time the face I saw looking back at me was my own. I felt a strange shudder pass through me, like an echo in the mind and in the body, as if I'd seen and felt this before. After the man disappeared I turned and ran up the bank and caught up with my brother and Muriel and her father. He asked what had put such a strange look on my face when he saw me. I told him the truth. I didn't know, I said. He helped me up the slope that rose to a field of black earth that stretched as far as the eye could see, deep into the heart of America. The soil was newly turned, judging by the smell of it, rich and manure-scented and still moist and cool from the night.

ACKNOWLEDGEMENTS

I am grateful for the financial support of the Canada Council for the Arts, the Ontario Arts Council, and the Toronto Arts Council.